"I've wanted t[...]
walked into th[...]
bride's outfit."

"It wasn't fancy," Leanne protested.

"You were beautiful in it," Cade said. "A dream come to life."

He touched her hair, startling her as he smoothed the tangles caused by the busy day. Electricity ran through her scalp and down her neck, lodging in the middle of her chest.

There was something in him, some breath-stealing darkness that called to something equally wild and restless within her, a quality she hadn't known she had until she'd stumbled into his hidden lair.

She didn't know why he made her feel this way, and it bothered her. No man had ever induced the pulsing sensations that throbbed inside her, demanding attention. It confused her. It made her angry.

And it excited her beyond all reason.

MONTANA MAVERICKS: WED IN WHITEHORN
Brand-new stories beneath the Big Sky!

MONTANA MAVERICKS

LAURIE PAIGE

says, "One of the nicest things about writing romances is researching locales, careers and ideas. In the interest of authenticity, most writers will try anything...once. I've interviewed fighter pilots, FBI agents and detectives. It's fun to investigate a burglary scene, ride a canoe through white-water rapids or climb on a glacier. Landing on a crystal-clear mountain lake in Alaska in a pontoon plane is exciting. I've donned a parachute harness and jumped from a simulation platform. I've ridden a horse, a cow, a donkey, a camel and a pig. But never will I hang-glide."

In addition to the above, she's been a NASA engineer, a past president of the Romance Writers of America (twice!), a mother and a grandmother (twice, also!). She was twice a Romance Writers of America RITA Award finalist for Best Traditional Romance and has won awards from *Romantic Times Magazine* for Best Silhouette Special Edition and Best Silhouette novel. She has also been presented with *Affaire de Coeur*'s Readers Choice Silver Pen Award for Favorite Contemporary.

Recently resettled in Northern California, Laurie is looking forward to staying in one place and is eager to experience whatever adventures her next novel will send her on.

MONTANA MAVERICKS

CHEYENNE BRIDE

LAURIE PAIGE

Published by Silhouette Books
America's Publisher of Contemporary Romance

Special thanks and acknowledgment are given to Laurie Paige for her contribution to the MONTANA MAVERICKS: WED IN WHITEHORN series.

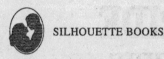 SILHOUETTE BOOKS

ISBN 0-373-65047-7

CHEYENNE BRIDE

Copyright © 2000 by Harlequin Books S.A.

Visit Silhouette at www.eHarlequin.com

Printed in U.S.A.

MONTANA MAVERICKS

Wed in Whitehorn

*Welcome to Whitehorn, Montana—
a place of passion and adventure.
Seems this charming little town has some
Big Sky secrets. And everybody's talking about...*

Leanne Harding: When the time came to say, "I do," her heart screamed, "I don't!" So she hitched up her skirts and hightailed it to her brother's ranch...where she met the man of her dreams. Only, he regarded her with outright disdain...and a whole lot of desire....

Cade Redstone: Funny, but mere months prior he'd been a jiltee, and now groom jilt*er* Leanne was seeking solace on the ranch where he worked. He knew he should hate her, but the true-blue cowgirl made it nearly impossible once he learned why she couldn't marry the wrong man...and how much he wanted her himself.

Christina Montgomery: Recent lore says Whitehorn water is increasing the population by sips and booties. But suspected mommy-to-be Christina seems awfully sad....

Blake Remmington: Secret heirs aren't sprouting solely in the Kincaid family tree. Seems daddy Remmington is about to be reunited with Junior....

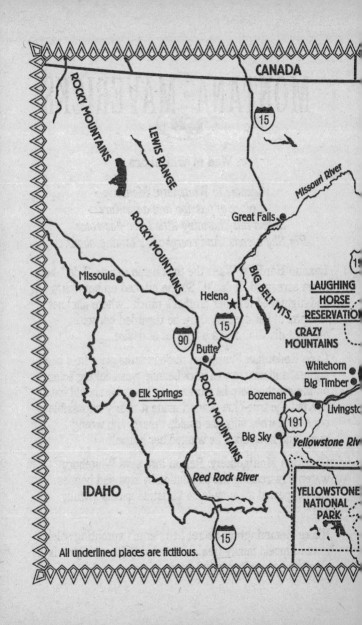

All underlined places are fictitious.

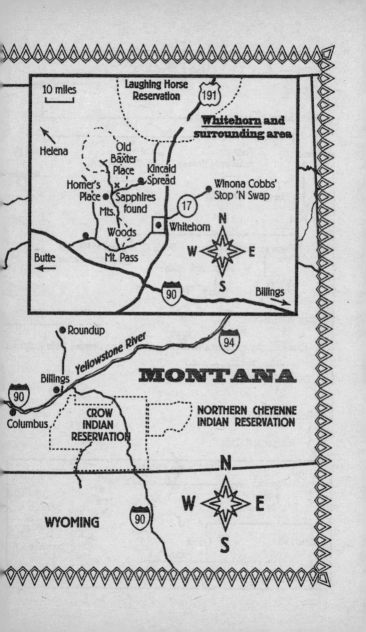

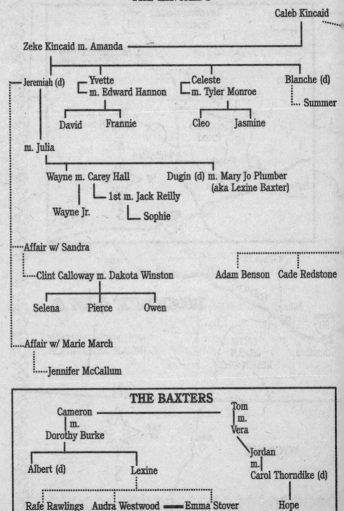

MONTANA MAVERICKS: WED IN WHITEHORN
THE KINCAIDS

Caleb Kincaid

Zeke Kincaid m. Amanda

Jeremiah (d) — Yvette m. Edward Hannon — Celeste m. Tyler Monroe — Blanche (d)
··· Summer

David   Frannie   Cleo   Jasmine

m. Julia

Wayne m. Carey Hall   Dugin (d) m. Mary Jo Plumber
(aka Lexine Baxter)
└ 1st m. Jack Reilly

Wayne Jr.   └ Sophie

····Affair w/ Sandra

····Clint Calloway m. Dakota Winston   Adam Benson   Cade Redstone

Selena   Pierce   Owen

····Affair w/ Marie March

····Jennifer McCallum

THE BAXTERS

Cameron ——————— Tom
m.   m.
Dorothy Burke   Vera

                  Jordan
                  m.
Albert (d)   Lexine   Carol Thorndike (d)

Rafe Rawlings   Audra Westwood ═══ Emma Stover   Hope

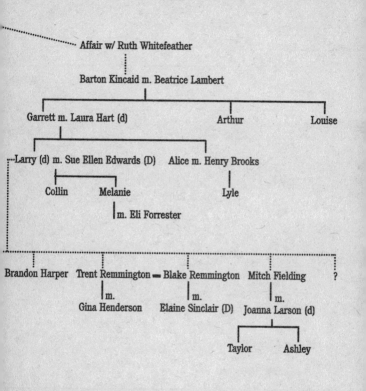

Affair w/ Ruth Whitefeather

Barton Kincaid m. Beatrice Lambert

Garrett m. Laura Hart (d)   Arthur   Louise

Larry (d) m. Sue Ellen Edwards (D)   Alice m. Henry Brooks

Collin   Melanie   Lyle

m. Eli Forrester

Brandon Harper   Trent Remmington ━ Blake Remmington   Mitch Fielding   ?

m.   m.   m.
Gina Henderson   Elaine Sinclair (D)   Joanna Larson (d)

Taylor   Ashley

Symbols
..... Child of an Affair
━━ Twins
d   Deceased
D   Divorced

One

Cade Redstone pulled his mount to a halt on the trail at the edge of the woods. Protected from the wind by the trees, he surveyed the broad meadow below. To think that part of it was his...or would be if the sale of the ranch went through as his newly found grandfather hoped.

That he, a cowboy, dreamer of impossible dreams and former champion calf-roper, would be a one-sixth or one-seventh owner of the Kincaid spread of Whitehorn, Montana—according to whether his biological father had sired six or seven illegitimate sons—totally blew his mind.

He'd been saving every penny for years to buy into his own place. And now this...

The wind surged down from the Crazy Mountains, stirring the fir trees, setting the Appaloosa to sidestepping, and sending shivers down his neck. He heard the first drops of rain hit the woods with a sharp rat-a-tat-tat.

He pulled the waterproof slicker from under the straps on the back of the saddle and slipped it over his head. After tucking an edge under each leg, he adjusted his hat to a more secure position and, lowering his head against the wind, headed for the cabin at the far side of the pasture where three hundred head of beef grazed in the deepening twilight.

The rain turned to a combination of sleet and hail before he was halfway to his destination. The wind was icy cold. This was January weather back in Gilas, near San Antonio, where he hailed from.

Welcome to July in Montana.

Cade reached the clearing just as the heavens opened up in a deluge that obscured everything more than ten feet away. He led the horse around the cabin and into a lean-to. There he unsaddled Stepper, named because he had a high, showy way of prancing, and wiped him down with a burlap sack. He broke a hay bale apart and tossed half of it into the manger. Stepper whinnied his approval and began chomping on his supper.

"Yeah, I'm hungry, too," Cade said, hanging the sack to dry on a nail. "It's been a long day."

But he'd wanted to see the land for himself, alone, to smell it and study it, hell, to taste it if he wanted, with no one to laugh at his foolishness. He'd drunk from a mountain spring, so cold and pure, it was better than champagne. Not that he was much into fine wines. He was mostly a beer-and-peanuts man.

Dashing around the corner of the building, he entered the rough cabin and lit the kerosene lamp. Good, there was firewood.

He flung his coat and slicker on a hook near the door and tossed the saddlebags on a chair, then checked the damper and started a fire in the potbellied stove. The thing looked old enough to have been the original one invented by Ben Franklin, but it drew air just fine. Soon he had a crackling fire going.

The pantry was well-stocked with soup, assorted beans and a variety of canned or dried meat. There was a plastic container of crackers and a half full-bottle of whiskey. Four bunk beds occupied one wall, complete with plastic-covered foam pads for mattresses. A chest contained wool blankets. All the comforts of home.

He mixed a can of beef stew with one of lentil soup in a beat-up pan and set it on the stove to heat. He filled a teakettle from a hand pump on a well beside the cabin door. He could make a cup of coffee after dinner, then use the rest of the hot water to wash up before bed.

All the comforts of home except a hot shower and an indoor bathroom, he amended after he ate. He poured up the coffee, left it to cool, and headed for the outhouse set well behind the cabin after pulling on his coat and slicker again. The rain was coming down in buckets.

Leanne Harding stared at the dirt road barely visible through the gloom and rain. She had a feeling she'd taken a wrong turn somewhere on this mad journey.

She should have been at the Kincaid ranch by now. She'd been to the place several times since her brother, Rand Harding, had taken a job there as the foreman.

Her plan was to hide out in his house for a while. She knew he wasn't home. Rand, his wife Suzanne, Joey, their baby, and Mack, Suzanne's teenage brother, were in Ox Bow to attend a wedding. Hers.

The white lace on her wedding dress fluttered as she sighed in despair. Why had she run away?

She had panicked, pure and simple. Her family was going to be furious with her. A quiver of despair trembled deep inside her at the thought. Some people thought she was flighty and spoiled. Right now she worried they might be right.

Was that a light up ahead? She peered through the driving rain that fell faster than the wipers could swish it away from the windshield. Yes! A ray of hope glowed in her.

It wasn't the Kincaid ranch quarters, but it was shelter from the storm. She pulled her compact car under the branches of an old oak tree at the end of the road. Grabbing her overnight case, she scrambled out and ran across the stubby grass toward the house.

Thank goodness the door wasn't locked. She was drenched and cold and shivering by the time she got it closed and was securely inside. She quickly surveyed the room, then went back over it more thoroughly.

No one was there, but a pan and a teakettle bubbled on a stove, which emitted the most wonderful warmth. She moved closer to it.

Her stomach growled at the aroma coming from the pan. She found a generous serving of soup in it. A cup of coffee, still steaming, was on the wooden table.

The hair stood up on the back of her neck.

She felt like Goldilocks exploring the cabin of the three bears. The weather, however, wasn't conducive to a walk in the woods while waiting for their porridge to cool. So where was the person who had prepared his supper and a cup of coffee and then disappeared?

She wondered why she thought the absent owner was a male. Because no sane female would be caught dead out on a night like this, she told herself with a wry attempt at humor.

Her amusement fled when she caught sight of herself in an old mottled wall mirror. Her hair straggled around her face. The arc of white roses and baby's breath attached to a froth of gossamer veil was wilted. The bridal wreath tilted drunkenly toward one side of her head.

Her wedding dress was ruined. Mud stained the hem of the heavy cream satin. Tears filled her eyes.

Taking a deep breath, she tried to hold the useless emotions in check. She was twenty-six years old and she was as unsure as she'd been at sixteen and in the unhappy throes of her first big case of puppy love—

The door burst open just as a clap of thunder broke over the cabin and reverberated between the mountain peaks that surrounded them like a thousand marching drummers. She gasped as a dark apparition entered the cabin and slammed the door.

Leanne remained frozen in place while the intruder hung up his hat, rain slicker and a sheepskin-lined denim jacket. She had an impression of darkness as he pushed black hair off his forehead. His eyebrows were thick and dark, shading deep-set eyes that seemed as black as the storm-driven night. His skin was deeply tanned, as if he spent a lot of time outdoors.

He was also brawny, at least six feet, with wide shoulders and muscular arms that flexed under a blue plaid work shirt as he leaned against the wall and tugged his boots off. He neatly lined them up against the wall and padded toward the table in his socks. Then he stopped.

Leanne held her breath.

His gaze swept over the cabin and landed solidly on her. She felt his antipathy in the piercing silence that surrounded them while they stared at each other.

"You just passing through or are you staying awhile?" he asked in a steel-tinged baritone.

"Staying." She surprised herself at how determined and certain she sounded. As if she knew what she was doing.

"How'd you get here?"

"Car. It's under the tree at the end of the road."

He grunted and settled at the table. He studied her over the rim of the heavy white cup as he took a drink.

She folded her arms and waited, ignoring her hunger and the sudden fear that he would cast her out into the night. She realized she was more afraid of that than of him. Which was probably the craziest of the insane thoughts she'd had that confusing, disappointing and dreary day.

Dizziness washed over her. She hadn't eaten anything all day but a piece of toast that morning. Her stomach growled again. Embarrassed, she placed a hand over it.

"You'd better sit before you fall," he said, rising. "There's some soup left."

She did as he advised. In less than a minute a big bowl of lentils and beef was in front of her. He placed a plastic container of crackers on the table.

"Dig in."

She did, aware of his disapproving scrutiny while she scraped the bowl clean. He opened a can of peaches and a package of cookies. She thought she could have eaten the whole thing, but he doled them out equally. He made a cup of instant coffee and plunked it down at her place, then refilled his own cup. She sighed when she had eaten the bowl of peaches and four cookies. She was tired to the bone.

"Okay," he said in a businesslike manner, "tell me who you are and what you're doing out in these parts in that get-up." He motioned toward her bedraggled wedding outfit.

She sighed again. "My name is Leanne Harding."

"Kin to Rand Harding?"

"Sister."

She saw the light dawn in his eyes. "He's gone to his sister's wedding over in Ox Bow."

"I—I left before the ceremony."

She thought of Rand and Suzanne, her sister Daisy, the wedding guests.... With a guilty start, she realized she hadn't thought much about Bill at all.

"Why?"

"I realized I couldn't go through with it." She bit into her bottom lip while she sought words to explain. "It seemed all wrong..."

"A little late to be thinking along those lines."

His tone hardened. It felt like a whiplash cracking over her taut nerves. She glanced at him and saw contempt in his eyes. She looked away. Whatever he thought couldn't be half as terrible as she felt about herself.

She could imagine the anger and humiliation she

had left in her wake. "There's nothing you can say that I haven't already said to myself," she told him, the misery rising to the surface and misting her eyes.

"It's nothing to me. I just feel sorry for the poor slob you left at the altar."

"No, I didn't. I mean...I told him before we went to the church. I found out— Well, it doesn't matter. But then I couldn't...I was so shocked and disappointed that he'd bought a house instead of the ranch—"

She realized she wasn't making much sense. She sighed as the disappointment rushed over her again, just as it had when Bill's sister, who couldn't keep a secret in a locked vault, had told her he'd bought a house for them in town, near the country club. Without asking her. Without her seeing it. As if her opinion didn't count.

All her dreams, all the plans they'd made, had shattered in an instant as she realized he'd never meant to buy the small ranch they'd looked at. "I gave him all my savings and part of the inheritance from my parents. Twenty thousand dollars. I trusted him..."

Her lips trembled. She pressed them together.

"You gonna cry?" her host asked, his tone dry as day-old toast.

Not trusting her voice, she shook her head. She'd rather die than break down in front of this hard-hearted stranger. "Thank you for the meal," she said politely. "I'll be on my way. Could you tell me where the Kincaid place is and how to get to the foreman's house?"

Cade studied the bride in her stained finery. The dress was sort of old-fashioned, with long sleeves and beads over the bustline. It fit real nice up top, then slid gracefully down her slender figure to her toes. In the back, it was gathered into a fold, like a bustle, and swept to the floor in a short train. A wilted wreath sat at a rakish angle on her head. Her dark hair picked up red highlights in the lantern light.

She looked miserable, and well she should, standing a guy up at the church. But even as his contempt rose, he had to admit to a stirring in his body. His unwanted guest was beautiful, if a trifle frazzled.

"You'll never make it in the dark," he advised. "You passed the turnoff from the main road a few miles back. Now you're in the back country. That was an old mining road you followed. It's too dangerous to navigate at night."

Her wide green eyes sparkled in the lamplight, and he realized she was near tears. Her fingers shook slightly when she lifted the coffee cup to her lips. He wondered about the chump she'd left behind.

Bitter anger flashed through him like heat lightning. He knew how that felt. Donna, his one-time fiancée, had gotten cold feet at the last minute and left him at the altar, quite literally.

Luckily it had been a small wedding with only their folks and closest friends in attendance. Feeling like the biggest fool that ever lived, he'd had to tell everyone they had changed their minds. He'd made a joke of it, but it had hurt. He'd made sure no one realized how much, including his fiancée's weeping mother.

Women. Who needed them?

"Is it okay if I spend the night?" she asked.

He exhaled heavily. "Do we have a choice?"

* * *

"Here."

A tanned hand thrust a pan of steaming water behind the blanket suspended on a rope between two nails. Leanne quickly took the water and set it on a wooden chair, trying once more to release the tiny hooks at the back of her dress.

"Uh," she said out loud to get his attention. He hadn't told her his name and, for some reason, pride refused to allow her to ask. "I, uh, need some help. I can't get the hooks on this dress undone."

She heard another heavy sigh, then the blanket was jerked aside. "Turn around," he snarled.

"I got the zipper, but the hooks are stuck or something," she explained in carefully reasoned tones.

She was used to explaining herself to her family. They loved her, even indulged her "whims," as they called them, but everyone thought she needed lots of direction. They called her dreams "flights of imagination." No one considered them very practical.

She blinked away tears as she obediently turned her back to her host. The space seemed smaller as he moved closer, then took hold of the cream satin. She shivered as his fingers brushed her spine.

"The hooks are tangled in a bunch of threads. I don't see the wire loops they're supposed to hook onto."

"The threads are the loops. The material is supposed to lie smoother that way."

"Huh," was his succinct comment.

As he bent close, she felt his breath on her back. She peered over her shoulder to see what he was doing. A frown of concentration creased two lines over the bridge of his nose, which was thin and sharply chiseled.

"Are you Native American?" she asked.

He glanced up and met her eyes. His probing glance caused her heart to beat furiously, like a butterfly trapped in a web. His fingers touched her back again, raising chill bumps.

"Half," he told her, his face expressionless. "My mother is Cheyenne. There's a little Mexican sloshing around in the background, too."

"Uh, you haven't told me your name."

He was silent for so long, she decided he wasn't going to tell her now, either.

"Cade Redstone. One of the long-lost bastard sons," he finally replied.

"I thought you must be one of Larry Kincaid's offspring. You have the Kincaid look and manner. Haughty."

She was appalled at herself for the insult. She pressed her lips together, but it was too late to take the words back. She retreated a wary step.

To her amazement, instead of anger, Cade burst into laughter. Even more amazing was the change in his expression. She'd thought he was handsome in a moody, exotic way, but his smile transformed his face, disclosing white, perfectly aligned teeth and, most amazing of all, a dimple indenting one cheek. Lines etched the corners of his eyes, indicating he had once laughed often.

But that had been in the past. Somehow she knew he no longer found life amusing.

"Hold still or we'll be here till midnight," he ordered, bending to the task once more. ''There're about a thousand threads caught on the hooks.''

''Cut them,'' she said, again aware of the warmth of his hands and the gentleness of his touch as he worked.

''In a minute.''

The weariness and the need to cry out the terrible tension of the day dissolved into a heightened sensitivity of her companion and the isolation of the cabin.

Taking a deep breath, she stared out the window into the darkness. The rain alternated with sleet and hail that banged against the glass in threatening waves.

When Cade gave an exasperated snort, she nearly jumped out of her skin as the heat of his breath seared right down to the point inside her where her nerves were coiled like a too tight spring.

''Relax,'' he said.

''I can't. I think I need to sit down. Please.'' She hated that the words sounded like a plea. She was coming apart, and that wouldn't do at all, not at all.

He moved the pan of water to the floor and pulled the chair around for her to sit. She did so gratefully.

''You're shaking.''

His tone was different—gruff but patient.

The tears welled again. ''It's been a long day.''

''And then some,'' he added, almost sympathetically.

Leanne looked over her shoulder again. His face was inches from hers. She could see tiny green flecks surrounding the pupils and the golden tones in the little valleys between the darker striations in the irises of his eyes. His eyelashes were short but very thick.

"You have kind eyes," she told him.

"Don't count on kindness from me," he advised coolly, the contempt returning.

She lowered her head against the finality of his rejection. "Cut the loops."

"All right."

When he clicked open a pocketknife, she sat very still and waited. She felt the cool edge of the metal against her skin, then the relaxing of the material as she was freed from the two tiny hooks set above the zipper of the dress.

The beaded top fell away from her breasts as the sleeves, which barely clung to her shoulders, slipped down her arms. She grabbed the bodice and held it tightly to her chest as heat flowed up her neck.

"Thank you," she said in a stilted tone. She was having an awful time finding an emotional level with this man.

"You're welcome," he said just as stiffly. He disappeared behind the blanket.

She removed the ruined bridal dress, the sheer thigh-high stockings and white satin bikini briefs. She washed as quickly and quietly as possible, then donned the white lace gown and robe from her overnight case.

What a farce, she mused as she tied the tasseled belt. No husband would see her tonight. Guiltily she wondered if Bill was sleeping in the new house he'd bought. They'd agreed not to spend money on a honeymoon.

Resentment rose in her. When Bill had said he had a terrific surprise for her on their wedding day, she hadn't suspected a house in the trendy part of town.

Anger overrode both the guilt and resentment. When was she going to be treated like an adult rather than the baby of the family who couldn't make a decision?

Realizing her fiancé treated her the way her family did had been the straw that had overturned her control and sent her scurrying for sanctuary.

Hearing Cade Redstone fill his coffee cup again, she had to smile at the irony of the situation. Her host didn't want any part of providing a haven for her. That reminded her...

"Uh, Mr. Redstone." That sounded ridiculous. "Cade?"

"Yeah."

"Would you please not tell my brother I'm here, if he calls?"

There was a frigid silence before he spoke. "Since there's no phone, I don't see a problem."

"I meant, at the ranch. If he calls there. I'd rather no one know where I am until..."

Until when?

"Until I sort things through and decide what I'm going to do," she finished stoically.

"I don't lie for anybody."

A flat statement delivered in a deadpan tone. She nodded in understanding as she stepped from behind the makeshift curtain.

His eyes opened in a brief flash of surprise before his face settled into such stern, disapproving lines he would have done an old-time tent preacher proud while he shouted condemnation on the sins of his congregation.

"It's all I have," she apologized, gesturing toward her outfit. "My suitcases were already in Bill's car."

He muttered an expletive and surged to his feet, turning his back on her. She stood there uncertainly while he opened the stove and tossed in two pieces of wood, then grabbed the poker.

How much was a man supposed to take? Cade asked himself savagely while he built up the fire for the night.

First of all, he'd had to help her with her dress. When he'd finally gotten the damn hooks unfastened, the dress had slithered down, exposing one pink-tipped breast, small and succulent and perfectly shaped. Her nipple had beaded upon being exposed.

He cursed silently and long.

Then he'd had to listen while she washed up. Pictures of what she was doing flickered in his mind like a runaway movie projector. To top it all, she then appeared before him as a vision of every man's fantasy in her white silky gown and lacy robe that disclosed little but hinted at everything.

Her chestnut hair with its fiery highlights lay smoothly across her shoulders and down her back, ready to be tousled by an ardent lover. Her face had been scrubbed as clean as a cherub's, ready to be kissed. She looked wickedly innocent. Or innocently wicked.

His imagination ran wild.

The blood pumped hot and turgid through his body, bringing with it an ache that couldn't, wouldn't, be appeased. It was going to be a long night.

Hellfire, just how much did she think a man could take, stranded alone in an isolated cabin as they were?

With an effort, he pulled his libido back under control, although there was nothing he could do about the telltale ridge lining the fly of his jeans.

"I see you have cocoa," she said, nodding toward the table. "Would you mind if I made some?"

"Help yourself." His tone didn't invite further questions or requests.

He was aware of her movements as she spooned cocoa into a cup and added hot water from the kettle. The silk of her robe brushed his arm as she placed the teakettle back on the stove. "I'll get more water," he said.

He grabbed the kettle and headed out the door, only remembering he was in his socks when he felt the freezing rain soak through the material. He cursed some more as he pumped water into the kettle.

When he entered the cabin, she was tending the lantern. She turned the wick down a bit until it stopped smoking, then replaced the chimney. He'd meant to do that, but had gotten distracted by her appearance in that innocent enchantress outfit.

He set the teakettle on the stove none too gently, then stripped his socks off and hung them to dry on nails pounded into the wall behind the stove. She didn't say a word while he got dry ones out of his saddlebags.

Pausing, he peered at her pink-nailed toes winking out at him from the bottom of her robe. He tossed a pair of warm wool socks to her. "You'll need these."

She took a seat at the table and lifted the silky material out of the way while she pulled the socks on.

"That feels wonderful," she said, smiling up at him, her eyes shining as clear and green as a soda bottle in the lamplight. "My shoes are wet. And ruined," she added.

He ignored the sorrow in her eyes and yanked on another pair of socks. "Why did you come to the ranch?"

What he really wanted to know was whether this was a coincidence or if fate was being particularly unkind to him for reasons he didn't know.

She stirred the cocoa, her face thoughtful. "I knew Rand and his family would be gone for two weeks of vacation after the wedding. I didn't think anyone would dream of looking for me here. I left a note that I was going to a friend's house until…until I got my bearings and figured out what to do."

"Until the furor dies down," he corrected sardonically.

At the flash of sadness in her eyes, he paused in his condemnation. He hardened his heart against feeling sorry for her. Her life and its problems, whatever they were, were no concern of his.

She obviously wasn't mature enough for the responsibilities that marriage demanded. At any rate, she was probably more than any sane man should take on, in marriage or out.

Maybe it was better for the poor fool bridegroom that she had run out on him. Looking back at his own disastrous wedding attempt, he realized that was the case for him.

His fiancée had accused him of not loving her enough. She'd said he loved the land more. Her accusations had struck to the core of his being. Maybe the trouble wasn't with his loving, but with being lovable. Maybe no woman would ever love him enough to put up with him.

Or maybe he wanted too much.

His mother had set the example in his life. And still did. She worked with her man, pulling her own weight in the marriage and on the ranch. She was loyal and loving. And fun. She'd left her first husband—the man Cade had thought was his biological father—because he'd abused her. Then she went on to find her true mate in Judd Redstone. Back home in Gilas, Texas, their marriage was still going strong. That's what he wanted.

He studied his unwanted guest. Yeah, the guy was probably lucky she'd run out on him. But, he also had to admit, any man would be tempted to claim this little gal for his own. She was that seductive.

Two

Cade's disposition was definitely on the sour side the next morning. He had slept on the top bunk of one set of bunk beds. Leanne had slept on the bottom of the other set. He'd wanted as much distance from his unexpected guest as he could get, which wasn't much in a one-room cabin.

The fleeing bride had cried during the night. Quietly. Discreetly. But her frequent sniffs and deeply drawn breaths had given her away. She'd cried a long time.

Probably because she dreaded facing the music when her brother, not to mention the fiancé, both of whom would be furious and rightly so, caught up with her.

He almost felt sorry for her.

However, each time pity had reared its head he'd remembered how it had felt to be left standing at the altar, waiting and waiting until finally the maid of honor had brought a note that said his bride had decided she preferred the city to the country and was leaving for Houston, along with his ring and the new wardrobe he'd bought for her.

Better to know before the marriage than afterward. Only the foundation of the house he'd planned on his stepfather's land remained to remind him of his folly.

He'd even begun negotiations to buy a small adjoining acreage to start his own place. He'd dropped those plans, the beginnings of his dream, after the aborted wedding.

Looking out the window at the clouds still covering the small valley, he smiled. This was real and part of it was his. There was more than enough land for six or seven brothers to share. He had his grandfather, Garrett Kincaid, to thank for that.

"Uh…"

He turned at the sound. Leanne Harding stood in front of the makeshift curtain, looking like an angel in her gown and robe. His body hardened. That was nothing new. He'd spent most of the night in that condition.

"Yeah?"

"I don't have anything to wear," she said.

Even with reddened eyes and pink nostrils, she still looked beautiful. In the morning light, he saw her hair was a deep chestnut, with shiny red highlights cast generously throughout the thick, wavy strands.

"Sorry, I don't carry a full line of women's apparel with me."

She looked as if she might burst into tears. Her small white teeth bit into her bottom lip and stopped its trembling. Her chest lifted and fell in a silent breath. She looked totally miserable.

Against his better judgment, he went to his saddlebags. "Here," he said, pulling out a blue chambray work shirt and a clean T-shirt.

He took out his spare pair of jeans, which he'd planned to change into after a bath in the hot springs on the way back to the ranch. He tossed the items to her.

"I can't help you with shoes," he said dryly.

She nodded, sniffed, and disappeared behind the curtain. He tried to ignore the slight rustling sounds she made as she changed, but images kept leaping into his mind. The robe came off, then the silky gown slithered to the floor. He knew she wore no bra. He imagined her arms lifting and her breasts jutting out as she pulled the shirt on. He heard the zip of the jeans as she finished.

She stepped from behind the blanket.

He saw she'd threaded the tasseled belt from her robe through the belt loops of the jeans. The T-shirt was tucked inside the pants, the outer shirt left open at the front, its sleeves rolled up on her slender forearms.

"The oatmeal is ready," he told her.

"And bacon. Wow."

"It's from a can."

"And you made biscuits."

He grinned sardonically at her exaggerated wide-eyed amazement. "A man who doesn't learn to take care of his own needs is a fool."

She looked him over with those bottle-green eyes, rolled the sleeves up one more notch, then took her seat at the table. "Sounds as if you learned that lesson the hard way, cowboy. Who pulled your string?"

"My ex-fiancée," he heard himself admit, much to his surprise. His past wasn't something he discussed with anyone at any time.

She stirred a spoonful of lumpy brown sugar into

the oatmeal with a thoughtful frown. "Did she leave you at the altar?"

"Yes."

"I'm sorry."

The simple apology touched him in ways he thought he could no longer be touched. It hit to the quick of that secret place where his boyhood dreams had once lived. But now he was thirty-five years old, long past boyish ambitions.

He shrugged. "It doesn't matter."

She didn't respond but looked at him as if she knew about that secret place. They ate the simple meal quickly and quietly. He washed up the few dishes and put the blankets away.

"You think you can find your way to the ranch?" he asked, holding the door open.

She nodded. "I go back to the main road, turn left, then turn left onto the ranch road, which should be the next one down the pike."

"Yeah. The mining road is going to be slippery after all the rain last night. It's dangerous along that granite bluff..." He rubbed a hand over his face, then put on his hat. "I'd better drive you in."

"What about your horse?"

Cade grinned. "He knows his way to the ranch."

"Unlike certain others you won't name."

He reluctantly admitted he liked her sense of humor, which came through in spite of the unhappiness in her eyes. While he moved his tack from the lean-to and stored it in her car, he wondered about the fiancé who had, Cade gathered, bought a house without asking her.

Even *he* saw that was a mistake. A woman needed

to be consulted on her house. It was her nest, so to speak. He'd gone over every detail of the house plans with his future wife and changed everything to suit her. Not that it had done any good in the end.

He cursed as he led Stepper to the trail that wound over the ridge and down to the ranch east of them. He didn't want to think of the old days. His life was off on a new start. He meant to enjoy it to the max.

"Home," he ordered, and slapped the Appaloosa on the rump.

With a shake of its head, the horse took off, tail and mane flying in the morning breeze, the distinctive rump spots that marked him as an Appaloosa flashing in the dawn light.

"He's beautiful," said a soft voice beside him.

The bride looked different. Standing barefoot in the grass, the wind tousling the dark fiery locks, her face shiny clean and without even lipstick to mar its freshness, she looked like a country girl, not the bedraggled city sophisticate she'd appeared to be last night.

Yeah, well, looks were deceiving, as someone wiser than he once noted.

"Let's go." He held out his hand for the keys.

"I'll drive." She headed for the car, her overnight case swinging at her side almost jauntily.

He frowned in irritation. Women always had to assert their independence at the wrong damn time.

Once on the road, he had to admit she showed a competence that he hadn't expected. She navigated the dangerously slippery ridge with a combination of confidence and caution that he liked.

They arrived at the ranch without mishap—only to find the doors to Rand's house locked. Cade looked under all the flower pots and the welcome mat and over the door facing. No key. Next to him, Leanne sighed, then straightened her shoulders.

"This, as they say, doesn't seem to be my day. Why would he lock the door?"

"This house is close to the main road. There's been a rash of break-ins in the county lately." He considered for a minute, then added, "You can stay at the bunkhouse. There's plenty of rooms there."

This last he mentioned rather sarcastically. The Kincaid ranch supposedly had a curse on it. They had trouble finding cowboys who would work the place.

"Good. I need a job," she told him as they drove on down the ranch road.

"That was the next thing on the agenda. The ranch doesn't cater to deadbeats. Everyone has to earn his or her keep. The cook can use a helper."

She wrinkled her nose and had the nerve to tell him that wasn't the kind of job she liked.

"I want to work outside, with the cattle. Or horses. I'm good with both."

He snorted. "Riding the herd isn't like those old Clint Eastwood movies."

"Actually, I learned everything I know from all the Roy Rogers-Dale Evans movies on cable TV. That always seemed the ideal life to me—a man, a woman and a horse named Trigger."

He muttered a prayer for patience. "We don't have time for cowboy-crazed females, either. You cause any trouble and you're out of here, pronto. Got that?"

"I got it."

Her glance was resentful, but he didn't let it bother him. He knew from talking to Rand that the sister was twenty-six and the youngest of the three kids. As a child, she'd been indulged in her passion for horses with riding and roping lessons instead of the ballet and piano lessons her mother had wanted for her. As far as he could tell, she was a spoiled kid who'd never grown up.

Except physically.

She was all woman in that department. A jolt of current went down his back as the image of that perfectly formed breast sprinted unbidden through his mind.

He directed her to park under the long overhang beside the bunkhouse, built to shelter the cowboys' trucks from the blizzards that sometimes started in September and didn't let up until March or April. And sometimes May and June.

There were four private rooms in the downstairs section. He directed her to one of those, empty now that another of the cowboys had moved on, uncomfortable with the Kincaid curse and the problems caused by some joker named Baxter who thought he had a claim to the ranch and was holding up the closing of the sale.

"Cookie," he called.

An old man ambled into view. Of mixed Gilas-Latino descent and uncertain age, he'd hired on about the time Cade and the other five bastard half brothers had arrived.

"Yes?" the cook said, taking his own sweet time.

The man had an attitude but he was the best ranch cook Cade had ever run into. "Found you a helper. Seems Rand Harding's sister has decided to visit for a while."

Cookie looked Leanne over until she thought he saw every secret, crazy wish she'd ever harbored. His eyes, a curious mixture of brown and blue that contrasted sharply with his black hair and olive skin, crinkled at the corners. "I can use her. You know how to peel potatoes?"

"Yes," she admitted glumly. She hated to be ungrateful, but she equally hated cooking and household chores.

"Good. Cowboys want 'em at every meal. Now they can have them again."

She saw the sardonic smile light up Cade's dark good looks and a satisfied glint appear in his eyes. It was obvious he thought he'd done his duty by her and gotten her out of his hair at the same time.

"I'll put my stuff away." She took her overnight case to the assigned room, feeling tired and unwanted.

Grow up, she advised her bruised spirit. No one on the ranch cared a darn about her. Maybe it was better that way.

Her family loved her, but they had wanted to tell her what to do, especially her big brother, Rand. After their parents' deaths, he had taken over as head of the family, consoling her and Daisy while hiding his own grief. He'd handled all the problems and rarely demanded anything from his sisters during that sad time.

She wondered if that was why she'd agreed to marry Bill. As Rand's oldest and best friend, he'd been around all her life. She had felt the not-so-subtle pressure that it was time for her to "settle down." Marriage to Bill had seemed the next logical step.

She sat on the bed in despair, feeling the weight of

her family's disapproval yet again. Why was it she always seemed to disappoint them?

After getting Leanne settled, Cade talked to Garrett and Wayne about hiring her on to help the cook. He was aware that Garrett Kincaid—he had trouble thinking of the man as his grandfather—found the situation amusing. So did Wayne Kincaid, the ranch manager, who was also Garrett's cousin.

In the absence of the foreman, Wayne had okayed the additional help, but he'd made it clear the runaway bride was Cade's responsibility.

Immediately after lunch, Cade had headed for the bunkhouse to check on her. Still in his clothing, she'd been busy at the stove, frying up a huge pan of hash browns in bacon drippings. She'd given him a severe frown, then had spoiled it by grinning at him.

Now, four hours later, leaning on the pasture fence where the spring foals frolicked near their moms, he still felt the effects of that bright smile. He laid a hand on his chest where his heart suddenly beat fast and furious.

She was an enigma, this woman who had blown into his life with the storm heralding her arrival. She was going to cause tumult in his life. He just couldn't say how yet.

A car appeared on the ranch road. He turned and watched Leanne as she parked and climbed out. Cade gritted his teeth as she bent and gathered several packages in the back seat.

The new ranch hand had gone shopping in White-horn. She was now dressed in snug jeans that neatly cupped her shapely rear. She wore an open cowboy shirt over a blue T-shirt. A gray Stetson, set at a jaunty angle, shaded her face from the summer sun, and sneakers protected her feet from the gravel on the road.

"Hi," she called. "I have your clothes all washed and ready to return." She brought them over. "I took them to the laundry. Was light starch okay?"

He took the package. "In my jeans?"

"Your shirt. I don't think they starch jeans and T-shirts."

Her smile was droll and somewhat mocking. He felt himself warming to it, and put on a stern face. "Isn't it time to start the next batch of potatoes?"

She wrinkled her nose. "I peeled two dozen before I left for town, so I'm ahead. For one meal. Don't you have some cows that need herding or something?"

He ignored the wistful look in her eyes. "No. Wayne Kincaid has approved your working here. There're some forms you need to fill out, and we need your social security number." He eyed her packages. "Meet me in the office in five minutes."

"Aye, aye, sir," she said smartly, and headed for the bunkhouse, packages swinging from both hands.

Smart-mouth female, he grumbled as he headed for the office, feeling only slightly guilty for not helping her with the packages. She might be his responsibility, but he wasn't going to cater to her.

After the forms were filled out, he left her in the kitchen slicing potatoes into home fries and headed for the newly built horse arena. He was completing the work in the tack and storage rooms himself. He knew exactly how he wanted them laid out.

When he'd presented his plans for the new Appaloosa line to Garrett and Collin, the one legitimate son of Larry Kincaid, they had approved it at once. Cade was now in charge of the horse breeding and training program on the ranch.

They had worked out an arrangement in which he would buy the horses needed to establish the line and the ranch would provide the quarters. He would do the training while the ranch supplied the feed. The profits from sales were to be shared equally between him and the ranch. The deal suited him just fine.

Working alone, he continued culling the remuda for those horses he wanted to keep and those the ranch could sell. He observed the yearlings and two-year-olds as well as the spring foals. Using a can of bright orange spray paint, he marked the keepers. The rest, when he finished, would be sold at auction later that month.

He grimaced at the work still to be done. They had already sent flyers to all the ranchers in the area, plus some of the big spreads down in Gilas. Cookie had been alerted to prepare a big barbecue.

That brought him back to Leanne. She could be of help during the auction, but he doubted she would be around that long. Although she came from a ranch and acted as if she knew about animals, he doubted she'd ever done much work in her life. Besides, flighty females weren't to be counted on.

"Ah, the Appaloosa," a feminine voice said behind him.

He jerked around, irritated that he hadn't heard Leanne approach.

"I was worried about him getting back to the

ranch, but I see he made it,'' she continued, her gaze on the horse that grazed in a nearby paddock.

"He's been trained to return to headquarters."

Cade winced at his harsh tone. He couldn't seem to find an equilibrium around this woman. He was too darn aware of everything about her, such as a subtle perfume wafting around her. She smelled good enough to eat. And looked that way, too.

Her eyes were no longer red. Free of all makeup, her face had a wholesome freshness that was pleasing. Her hair glistened in the sun. Little strands curled around her face and neck while the rest was swept up on top of her head.

He wanted to nuzzle his way down her neck, to smell and taste her skin, which was smoothly tanned with only an occasional golden freckle—

Damn! He had to stop thinking along those lines. He looked away with an effort.

The heat of late afternoon lay over the ranch, which was tucked into its own lush valley between the mountains. Two cowboys drove a fractious herd to a new field and closed the gate behind them. The men headed for the stable.

"Cookie give you some time off?" he asked.

She sliced him a sideways glance. "Supper is ready and on the table. He told me to ask if you were eating with the cowboys in the bunkhouse or at the main house."

"The bunkhouse," he decided. "Cowboys tend to be young and lonely. I'm supposed to keep an eye on you."

She spun and walked off, clearly angry with him.

He suppressed a need to apologize for the implied

insult. With quick strides, he closed the distance between them. "You're an attractive young woman. They're men. I don't want any trouble."

"Maybe they aren't like you," she said coolly.

"How's that?"

"Lecherous."

He had to smile. "That's the second time you've done that," he drawled.

Her stride didn't falter as she marched with grim purpose toward the dining room on the lower floor of the building. "Done what?"

"Turned the tables on me. Last night you called me haughty. Today, it's lecherous."

She turned to him, her eyes mockingly wide. "Wonder what tomorrow will bring?" She walked inside and let the door swing closed in his face.

"It won't be anything good," he muttered, still worried about his reactions to her as he went inside.

The few hands the ranch had were seated around the table, which could accommodate three times their number. They had already filled their plates and had dug in. A roast held pride of place on the long sideboard, along with green beans, creamed corn and a huge platter of home-fried potatoes and onions, which were Leanne's contribution. Rolls, salad and a banana pudding completed the meal.

Cookie ate in the kitchen, but Leanne, after getting a glass of tea and filling a plate, sat at the table. Cade took a chair beside her. He caught several cowboys glancing at her then him, speculation in their eyes. He wondered if he needed to make it clear she was under his protection until her brother arrived.

He took a deep breath. He had a gut feeling that

two weeks were going to seem like forever, and his nights were going to be disrupted by dreams he didn't want or need.

Hell, he'd always been a sucker for sweet-faced gals and a sob story.

Three

"Hey, come on, you'll enjoy it."

Leanne paused in cleaning up the breakfast dishes and peered worriedly at Gil Watts, the cowboy who was urging her to join the rest of the hands at the big Fourth of July celebration at the Laughing Horse reservation. She wasn't sure her warden, alias Cade Redstone, would approve.

"You can go with me," Cookie spoke up. "We ain't gonna feed these no-good bums any more today."

Within twenty-four hours of arriving, Leanne felt like a fixture at the ranch. After getting through lunch and dinner without mishap yesterday, the men had accepted her as one of them. The cook, who occupied the other downstairs bedroom in use at the time, evidently thought he was her keeper when Cade wasn't around.

"So, you gonna come with us?" Gil demanded.

She was curious about the residents of the reservation and interested in their culture. Cade was half Cheyenne. That was his heritage, too, the same as being a Kincaid. He would probably be there.

Her heart pounded furiously at the thought, startling her. Each time she'd seen him around the ranch yesterday, it had done the same thing. The habit was worrisome and irritating.

When she and Cookie finished cleaning the kitchen, she went to her room and changed to white slacks and a red top that tied at her waist. She put on a strong sunblock and a light touch of makeup.

The men were piled into one truck. Gil told her to hop in. She saw he had saved a place in the cab for her, but there was no place for Cookie.

"I'll drive my car," she called. "See you there."

Cade came out of the arena structure. From the disapproval on his face she figured he'd heard the cowboys' arguments.

"She's coming with me," he told the men as he strode across the gravel road and stopped beside her.

Gil looked angry, but left off cajoling her to join them. Cookie came out of the bunkhouse, saw the empty seat in the pickup and climbed up beside Gil, who drove off with a scowl.

"It'll take me a few minutes to shower and change," Cade said. "I've been working with the horses."

"I prefer to drive myself. I saw the reservation on my way here. I know where it is."

"Fine. I'll ride with you." With that, he walked off.

She made a face at his back.

"Hope you don't freeze like that," he said without looking around.

Surprised, she burst out laughing. "I knew you were weird, but I didn't think it extended to eyes in the back of your head."

He gave her a wicked glance over his shoulder.

"Haughty, lecherous and now weird. Interesting traits, huh?"

Very interesting, she mentally agreed, watching his long-legged stride to the main ranch house. He had lean hips and muscular legs that balanced his upper body very nicely.

Realizing she was staring at him—okay, at his superb body—she mused on the way her heart pounded when she saw him and the fact that she experienced the oddest tingles in the deepest part of her being and that her breath grew short when she was around him.

All the signs of falling in love, if romance books and fairy tales were to be believed.

But how could that be when only two days ago she was set to marry Bill Sutter? Maybe she was flighty as her brother had often accused. Tears burning her eyes, she hurried to her car as if a stampeding herd were on her heels.

Turning on the air conditioner to full-blast, she drove to the main house and waited for Cade under the shade of an ancient cottonwood. He joined her in ten minutes.

"Add 'fast' to the list," she said, striving for a light note. "Haughty, lecherous, weird and fast."

"At least in the shower," he drawled. "And if you spread that around, people are going to wonder how you know and maybe think you're a bit fast yourself."

It was a challenge she couldn't refuse. She tossed him a daredevil grin. "I've never much worried about what other people think."

"Sometimes words can hurt as much as sticks and stones," he said on a more thoughtful note.

She thought about his life. The newspapers had been filled with stories on the Kincaid brothers, legitimate and otherwise. "Were you taunted as a child?"

"No. My mother was married when I was conceived. Her first husband was abusive. Larry Kincaid gave her the money to leave him. She was the housekeeper at the Kincaid place at that time. She moved to Gilas and eventually married Judd Redstone, who became a real father to me."

"He sounds like a super person."

"The best."

A warm tingle went through her at the gruff emotion in his voice when he spoke of his stepfather. She added *loyal* and *loving* to the list of descriptive words for Cade.

They arrived at the Laughing Horse reservation in time for the opening ceremony—a parade of Native American men in full battle colors riding down the central corridor of the fairgrounds.

Leanne and Cade joined up with the other cowboys from the Kincaid spread. They tried their skill at the ring toss and bowling pins. And lost.

"Hey, shootin' is my game," Gil declared, leading the way to the rifle range kiosk. Ducks, bears and figures of other wildlife paraded back and forth among miniature trees and bushes. "Anyone want to take me on, a dollar for every time one of us misses?"

No one did.

"Come on, Redstone," he dared. "You got any moxie?"

"Maybe," Cade said in the laid-back Gilas drawl

he sometimes used, "but I left my shooting eye at the ranch."

This brought a chuckle from the other men, that seemed to defuse the tension. Leanne realized Gil had continually challenged Cade since they had arrived.

The male ego on display, she mocked silently.

"Bunch of chickens," Gil scoffed.

"Show us your stuff," one of the other men spoke up.

Gil tossed his money down and selected a rifle. He lined up his first shot and hit it dead-on. He proceeded to demolish all the targets. "I'll take that big teddy bear," he said, laying the gun down.

"Darn good shooting," Cade told him. "Glad I didn't let myself get suckered into a bet."

Gil preened under the compliment. He presented the three-foot-tall, pink-and-white bear to Leanne. "To the prettiest little gal to ever set foot in Montana."

Leanne couldn't refuse the gift. It would have been too great an insult to the cowboy. "Why, thank you, Gil. That's very kind of you."

"Nah," Cookie declared. "He jus' wants you to keep fixin' those potatoes."

Gil frowned as the men laughed. As a group, they toured the display booths lining the grounds. Leanne admired the pottery and blankets and wished she had some money. She'd used her credit card to buy clothing and was afraid to spend any more. She had no idea how much she would be paid by the ranch and was too proud to ask.

"Oh-h-h," she crooned when she saw the jewelry display at the next booth. "What are these?"

"Sapphires," the young Native American manning the display answered. "They come from around here. I search the stream beds for them. The miners used to find them when they were digging in the mountains for gold and silver. There's supposed to be a lost mine somewhere on the old Baxter place up near the Crazies."

"The Crazy Mountains," Cade clarified when she cast a puzzled glance his way.

"Wish I could find it," Gil said, pushing in beside Leanne, his hip touching hers. "They use sapphire lasers in some medical machines nowadays. Sapphires good for that are worth a fortune, I understand."

Leanne didn't like being crowded. She never had. Adroitly, she shifted her weight, angling away from the cowboy. She felt the immediate warmth of Cade's body along her other side. For some reason, touching him didn't bother her.

Because he wasn't coming on to her. Gil was.

She hid a wry smile and picked up a pendant. "This is beautiful. The color is so deep."

"It's radiated," the young Native American explained. "A lot of stones are almost colorless unless they're heated. You get this color with heating." He held up another necklace. "But radiation gives the deepest color."

"Doesn't that make the jewelry dangerous to wear?"

He grinned. "There's very little residual radiation, not nearly as much as a person gets on a sunny day outside."

She was aware of Cade pressing closer as he leaned over her shoulder. She glanced at him in surprise.

"Caleb Whitecloud," he said, picking up a business card. "You any kin to Bessie and Joe?"

The young man grinned. Like Cade, his smile changed his appearance, his teeth startling white against the dusky tones of his skin. There was a devil-may-care quality in his manner that reminded her of Cade at moments.

"Nephew," he replied. "Aunt Bessie makes the best fry bread on the res."

Cade held out a hand. "She's a cousin on my mother's side. Are we kin, too?"

Caleb shook his head as he clasped Cade's hand. "Uncle Joe's my blood relative. I don't recall seeing you around."

"I'm from Gilas, down around San Antone. This is my first visit up here. My mom used to tell me about her and Bessie's adventures here on the res."

"Aunt Bessie is handling the bead booth, on down about ten places, then turn left. She'll want to see you."

"Thanks. I'd like to meet her, too."

To Leanne's disappointment, Cade hurried off. Since she wasn't invited, she didn't go with him. That was the last time he was with the ranch group the rest of the day.

A couple of times she caught a glimpse of him with an older woman. Aunt Bessie, she assumed. The woman was introducing him to a group of Native Americans, some of which were very pretty females.

A hot, smothery sensation poured over her. She

wasn't jealous or anything like that, but...well, he rode with her. He could have asked her to join him.

The tribe displayed various types of ceremonial dancing later that evening. The tourists were invited to try some of them. Gil grabbed her hand and pulled her into the circle.

Without causing a scene, she had no choice but to go. Fortunately, the dance didn't call for him to hold her. Once she relaxed, she enjoyed moving to the rhythmic beat of the drums.

When some of the younger Native Americans formed a conga line, matching their movements to the increasing tempo, she was pulled into it. The elders frowned. Leanne grinned at the obvious clash between generations. It was the same in all cultures.

As the day faded into evening, the cowboys decided to head for the Black Boot, a bar on the outskirts of Whitehorn. She looked around for Cade, but he was nowhere to be seen. Fine. He could just find his own way home.

A jukebox was blaring out a song about a honkytonk woman, which Leanne thought entirely appropriate to the place when they arrived.

Gil, who'd been drinking beer all afternoon, ordered a round for them. She told the waitress firmly she wanted a soda. "Lots of ice," she requested. "I'm driving," she reminded the men. "So is Gil."

Cookie nodded. "I'll drive home. We're in a ranch truck. The Kincaids don't much like it when their men get in a wreck or arrested for drunk driving."

Gil looked as if he was going to argue, but changed his mind. Instead he clasped Leanne's wrist. "Let's dance."

"No, thanks." She made a circular motion with her arm and freed herself from his grip.

Gil grunted in surprise, then his face flushed dark red. Instead of cursing, he surprised her by smiling. "You too good for an ordinary ranch hand?"

Jimmy, the youngest cowboy hired for the summer, spoke up. "She doesn't want to dance."

Gil turned a mean gaze on him. "Who asked you, punk?" He raised a fist. "You want a taste of this?"

"If you think you can deliver it, go ahead and try," the cowboy challenged.

"Stop it," Leanne ordered. She threw a couple of singles on the table for her soft drink and stood.

Gil caught her around the waist. "Come on, sweetheart, just one dance."

"No."

"Let her go," a deep baritone drawled.

Leanne and the cowboys turned as a group. Cade grinned at them in his laid-back, insouciant manner. Relief washed over her as Gil let her go and stepped back.

"You ready to head in?" Cade asked politely.

"Yes." She glanced around. "How did you get here?"

"Caleb and his brother dropped me off."

"Oh, yes, you're newfound cousins." She couldn't stop the bite of sarcasm from seeping into her voice.

"Right," he said easily. "Goodnight, boys. See you at work bright and early tomorrow." With a grin, he led the way out of the bar.

Leanne breathed deeply of the fresh night air. She didn't know why she'd agreed to go to the bar in the first place. She hated smoke-filled rooms.

Cade climbed into the passenger seat of her car. She had expected him to demand to drive. Her brother would have gone right to the driver's seat, then lectured her all the way to the ranch on her rash behavior. Even though she adored Rand and knew he felt responsible for her, at times she wanted to tell him to shut up.

Her stomach went into a dive. She was going to have to face her family sooner or later. Later would be preferable, though.

Coward, her conscience admonished as she drove down the road to the ranch. Right. She also had the present moment to face up to.

"I was glad when you showed up. Sorry I got you into an awkward situation," she apologized to Cade. "I shouldn't have gone to the bar with the men."

"You should have been safe with them," he corrected. "It was their job to protect you. That includes respecting your wishes."

"That's probably an old-fashioned attitude in this day and age, cowboy," she said lightly.

Actually his words touched her. It was reassuring to be with a male who still thought it was his job to defend the female of the species. She felt cherished or…or something. She swallowed as a knot formed in her throat. She couldn't define what that *something* might be.

"Yeah, it's hard to be a hero with you independent women insisting on being treated as equals."

She broke into laughter as she realized he was teasing her. "But you would have helped a buddy who was being attacked by a bully, wouldn't you?"

"Only if it wasn't a fair fight. Where'd you learn to use that move to free yourself?"

"Tae kwon do self-defense class."

He whistled softly.

"I'm not a black belt, but I know some good moves."

Laughter rippled through his voice. "I've noticed."

Warmth spread through her like warm syrup on pancakes. Cade Redstone was endearingly unpredictable. Just when she thought he was going to come on as the stern older brother type, he surprised her with an entirely different attitude.

The sudden changes kept her off balance with him, never quite sure where she stood or what her reaction should be.

Except she hadn't mistaken the pure male interest in his eyes up at the cabin during the storm.

Her breasts tingled and the nipples beaded up into tight buds. With any other man, she might have been frightened at that incident, but not with this one. She'd known he was trustworthy from the moment he'd told her to sit down, then had set the soup and crackers on the table. He'd shared his dessert, too. And given her all the hot water.

How tired and full of despair she'd been Friday. With the wrong person, the night could have been a disaster....

Such as her fiancé?

"I'm glad I came to the ranch," she said slowly, thinking it out as she spoke. "The marriage would have been a terrible mistake. For Bill as well as me."

"How do you figure that?"

"I've realized I don't love him...actually, I do, but

as a friend, not a husband. I don't think he truly loves me, either. Rand wanted the marriage more than I did. He wanted me to settle down.'' She sighed. ''I think he felt he wouldn't be responsible for me if I was married.''

''You're over twenty-one,'' Cade pointed out.

''Tell that to my big brother.''

''What did you do before you lit out from your wedding like a scalded cat? Didn't you support yourself?''

''I worked in a farm and ranch supply store. I kept the books for them, and ordered the inventory after I got it all on the computer.''

''You good at using a computer?''

''Well, proficient at any rate.'' She parked under the overhang beside the bunkhouse. ''Why?''

''I'm setting up a breeding program to track the bloodlines of the new herd I'm starting. I could use some help.''

Her pulse beat a rapid drum song at the thought of working with him. The attraction between them reinforced the conviction that her feelings for her fiancé weren't what they should be. With Bill she'd never felt the awareness, the on-edge tingles she was experiencing now. With Bill sex had been embarrassing and uncomfortable. Already she knew making love with Cade would be passionate and thrilling. But why was she thinking such things? She'd only just met the man. Reining in those sexual thoughts, she returned to their conversation.

''Sounds interesting. I love working with animals,'' she added. That much was true, but it wasn't the only reason she was interested in the breeding program.

Worry ate at her as she realized she wanted to get to know this man, this wary rogue who was made up of so many intriguing parts.

His mouth kicked up at the corners. "Working with the horses isn't what I had in mind."

"I know," she said quickly. "But I'll be able to track them. Are you going to breed Appaloosas?"

"Yes, as riding and show ponies as well as cutting stock."

"Stepper will make a fine sire. His lines are perfect, and the color markings are beautiful."

Cade walked with her to the bunkhouse door. All the rooms within were dark. She realized all the men, including the cook, were off the ranch and she would be alone.

Cade opened the door and flicked on the lights in the dining room. "You afraid to stay here by yourself?"

"No. I feel safe at the ranch."

"Don't relax too much. You called me lecherous. Where you're concerned, you might be right."

He was smiling, but his eyes were serious. Like her, the attraction worried him. Tension zoomed straight up to the top of the scale.

"I think you might have noticed my reaction up at the cabin," he continued, his dark eyes roaming over her. "I've wanted to touch you since you walked into the cabin in that fancy bride's outfit."

"It wasn't fancy," she protested. "I made it."

"You were beautiful in it," he said, his voice dropping to a deeper register, his eyes settling on her face in moody hunger. "A dream come to life."

He touched her hair, startling her as he smoothed

the tangles caused by the busy day. Electricity ran through her scalp and down her neck, lodging in the middle of her chest. She had to open her mouth to breathe.

There was something in him, some breath-stealing darkness that called to something equally wild and restless within her, a quality she didn't know she had until she'd stumbled into his hidden lair.

She didn't know why he made her feel this way, and it bothered her. No man, including her fiancé, had ever induced the pulsing sensations that throbbed inside her, demanding attention. It confused her. It made her angry.

And it excited her beyond all reason.

He touched her neck, tracing a line along the vee of her shirt. "That dress...and then the silky night-gown...makes a man want to undress you slowly and see what surprises lie in store for him."

She gasped as pure energy flowed from the point where his fingers touched her to that wild, restless place inside. She wanted the surprises, too. Oh, heavens...

His eyes locked with hers. "You're shocked," he stated sardonically. "Now, that does surprise me."

"You didn't try anything." She bit the words off. Her voice came out strangled, choked with emotions she didn't understand. "You never indicated...except that one time...and your eyes, before then, when the dress slipped—"

"Yes," he said when she stopped abruptly. "When the bridal gown fell. No artist could conjure a more perfectly formed female shape. You'll never know the

willpower it took not to drop to my knees and take
my fill of you.''

''You were a perfect gentleman,'' she managed to
gasp.

''Was I? What about when you came out from that
blanket in the white silky gown and lacy robe? I
couldn't stop the reaction that time. You noticed,'' he
accused.

She couldn't look away from the dark intensity of
his gaze. The hunger was there again. And a certain
cynical knowledge in the smile that played around his
sharply etched lips. She couldn't hide the desire that
rose in her.

''Yes, but you didn't…never once did I feel threatened.''

''I'd never hurt a woman,'' he agreed. ''Or try to
force one who's unwilling.''

''What about seduction? Would you seduce one?''
She couldn't believe she'd asked such a stupid question.

''Who's being seduced?''

She couldn't lie or act nonchalant. ''Me. I think.''
Her heart pounded like a jackhammer, causing so
much racket she couldn't think.

''You?'' he questioned, the smile edging his lips
upward ever so slightly.

His finger traced the V-neck of her blouse, barely
touching her skin, which was suddenly hot, as if lava
flowed under its heated surface. A sheen of perspiration broke out over her.

''Or me?'' he continued on a deeper, quieter note.

''Both,'' she admitted. ''It was the circumstances,
the storm, the isolation…''

"And now? What is it now, if we both feel the same? The lingering aftereffects?"

She shook her head. She licked her lips, not nervous, but not sure what was happening, either.

He crooked his finger under her chin so she had to return his gaze. "I want to kiss you. Is that what you want?"

The thought hadn't consciously entered her mind, but now she realized she did. "Desperately."

His pupils widened. "Are you always so honest?"

"I don't know. It's different. Something is different. Because of you. I've never wanted like this."

A frown creased a tiny nick between his dark eyebrows. "Never, and you an almost-married woman?"

She shook her head. "It's confusing. I've never cared much for being touched."

He caressed her throat. "Like this? You don't like this?"

"No. I mean, I..." She took his hand in hers, stopping the tantalizing stroking. "I do like it. I don't want you to stop. I don't understand this at all."

"I'm a man. You're a woman. We're alone. That seems simple enough."

She cast him an upward glance from under her eyelashes. "You know that isn't all," she chided, disappointed that he would treat the situation so lightly.

He was silent for a long minute. "It's enough," he murmured. His breath caressed her a second before his lips did. "Give me your mouth," he said.

She opened her lips to him, unable to resist tasting just a little bit more of this hunger between them. She laid her hands against his chest and felt a shudder go all the way through his big masculine body; he wasn't taking the situation lightly at all.

It seemed miraculous that she could cause such a force in him. Or that he could cause such heat in her.

He tasted her mouth with his tongue, gentle at first, then more demanding. She returned the kiss, taking it deeper as she did the same to him. His hands clasped her shoulders and brought her closer.

She slid her arms around his back and held on as her legs grew weak with a passion she'd never experienced. It was strange to have never known this, and stranger yet to find it here in this place at this time.

"I'm melting," she warned him.

"Lean into me. You weigh no more than a sack of thistledown." His muscles rippled as he leaned against the door and pulled her into the vee of his legs.

The hard ridge outlined his zipper again. This time she got to feel it as well as see it. She moved experimentally back and forth. He groaned deep in his throat and kissed her again with savage tenderness this time. She answered with the same wild longing coursing through her.

She dropped her head back and closed her eyes as ecstasy swept over her. A whimpering sound forced its way out of her.

He stopped. She opened her eyes slowly and stared up at him, shaken by the tempest they had created. The moment grew and lengthened, until she saw a hardness descend over his face.

"You're a temptation." He stepped back and

dropped his arms to his sides. "And almost enough to make me forget my one foray to the altar. Almost." He walked off into the night.

Four

"Kincaid ranch." Cade answered the phone in his office as he frowned at the computer screen in annoyance. Trying to find information on the Internet was great when it went fast and easy. Other times it was frustrating.

"Who's this?" a male voice asked.

"Who are you calling?"

"This is Rand Harding," the foreman said impatiently. "Something's come up down here, a problem."

His brief laugh was sardonic. Cade tensed, sure that questions about the runaway bride were coming.

"My sister took off right before the wedding. We haven't heard from her since. She isn't at any of her friends' houses. Tell Kincaid—Wayne Kincaid—that I might not return on the fourteenth. In case I need more time to run her down."

His manner boded no good for the sister when he located her. Cade found himself feeling almost sorry for Leanne. She had a lot of music to face.

"She might show up at the ranch," Rand said, his tone expressing his doubts.

"In that case, I'll keep an eye on her," Cade promised.

That was certainly no lie. With young Jimmy smitten with her and trying to defend her from Gil, who wanted to score with her, he had to keep an eye on the situation. He should tell Rand to come and get her. But he didn't.

"There's a cabin in the mountains where my parents used to take us when we were kids. Bill and I are heading up there later today. Wayne has my cell phone number. He can call me if she shows up at the ranch."

"Right."

Cade hung up and tried to figure out why he hadn't told Rand everything. But the way he figured it, that was Leanne's job. She'd gotten herself into the mess and she could get herself out.

He headed for the dining room and a fresh cup of coffee. Trent Remmington—Larry Kincaid's fifth illegitimate son and three years younger than Cade— was there with Garrett. So was Trent's new wife, Gina—the P.I. who was still looking for Larry's reputed seventh son.

An interesting history their tomcat father had had. As far as Cade was concerned, Judd Redstone was his real father. The man had treated him every bit as much a son as he had Ryder, Cade's younger half brother.

"Good morning," Cade said to his new family.

"Cade." Garrett's voice brimmed with pleasure as it did each time he spoke to one of the Kincaid brothers, legitimate or not.

Cade felt himself warming to the patriarch the longer he knew him. Unlike his profligate son, the older Kincaid took his responsibilities seriously, hence his buying the Kincaid ranch in Whitehorn for his grandsons.

"Harding called this morning. I, uh, told him I would keep an eye on his sister. She says she knows computers. I'm thinking of having her set up the breeding records."

"Good idea," Garrett agreed at once.

Cade ignored the jabs from his conscience. This lying by implication about Leanne was getting too easy. He was letting the Kincaids think she'd quarreled with her fiancé and that her brother knew she'd come to the ranch to get herself together and rethink her life.

Which wasn't entirely a lie.

"Any new clues on the seventh son?" he asked Gina, who was prettily pregnant.

The brothers had razzed Trent about his fast work with the detective their grandfather had hired to find all the grandsons. He'd met, married and gotten her with child—not necessarily in that order—within a very short time.

"No. We're checking birth records at all the hospitals. It's a slow process."

"But we won't give up until we know for sure there's no child," Garrett put in.

Trent spoke up in a wry tone. "Never say quit. That's the family motto."

His eyes met Cade's in sardonic amusement. The brothers had, among themselves, remarked on their father's multiple brood. Apparently he'd been cast from the same mode as Jeremiah Kincaid, who, besides Wayne and a younger son, now deceased, had also had a couple of out-of-wedlock children.

Maybe it wasn't in the Kincaid men to be faithful. Looking at his grandfather, Cade knew that wasn't true. Maybe there was something within himself that wasn't capable of loving a woman, not enough to satisfy her....

"Well," he said, picking up the coffee mug, "I'd better get back to work."

He headed toward the room he'd set up as his office, but the day beckoned. The sun was shining. The sky was clear. He needed to be outside. He exited the side door and ambled over to the bunkhouse.

Cookie was putting a turkey in the oven. Leanne was icing a cake, making pretty rosettes around the edge.

"Hi," she said, pushing back a straggling curl with a lift of her shoulder. "We're making a birthday dinner for Jimmy. It's a surprise. Do we have candles?"

This last was said to Cookie, who grumpily informed her he didn't run a party store.

"I'll pick up some in town when I go this afternoon," she decided, undeterred from her quest.

"I have a job for you," Cade said in a hard voice, unsure how to act around her after that kiss a couple of nights ago. He'd managed to avoid her since then.

Her big green eyes stared at him warily, the bright humor of a moment ago gone. "Oh?"

"You said you could handle a computer. If Cookie can spare you, I want to get started on the breeding program."

"Take her," Cookie spoke up. "She drives me crazy, talk, talk, talk all the time."

She gave the old man a pretty pout, then turned to

Cade. "I'm almost finished here. Can you give me five minutes?"

He nodded and watched as she finished decorating the birthday cake with leaves around the roses. She washed up the utensils, dried her hands and turned to him.

"I'm ready."

"We need to go to town."

Surprised but pleased, she dashed to get her purse and fix her hair. The rubber band holding the thick tresses was gone when she returned. In its place was a green butterfly clip holding the side strands at the crown of her head.

He drove this time. She made no remarks on his old pickup and few about the scenery or weather on the way. He parked at the feed store and led the way inside. Along one wall was a shelf of computer programs especially designed for farmers and ranchers.

"You familiar with any of these?" he asked.

She looked the packages over. "A couple. Is there one you particularly like?"

"I don't know a thing about any of them. You said you used a computer for inventory. I figured the horses could be tracked the same way."

Her eyes sparkled up at him. "I used a spreadsheet and wrote my own macros. We can do the same. I tried to talk my dad into keeping up with his breeding herd like that, but he thought it was too complicated. Actually he didn't like the idea at all. But it should work great for horses," she finished on a positive note.

There was something totally honest in the way she admitted her father hadn't liked her idea.

"Poor little genius," he said.

Leanne laughed. His tone had been mocking, but gently so. He wasn't as mean as he liked to pretend. She trailed after him while he put in an order for feed for the horses, then talked to the store owner about delivery dates and the problems with wholesalers. The owner asked him for another brochure about the auction. He'd given the last one away.

After promising to fax another for the store bulletin board, Cade led the way outside. He glanced at his watch.

"It's lunchtime," he said. "You want to stop in town?"

"That depends."

"On what?" he asked irritably.

"On whether you're paying. I'm financially challenged at the present."

He cut a hard glance her way. "It's a loan. You get paid at the end of the week."

She smiled in relief. "Great. I wasn't sure I'd get anything besides room and board. How much am I making?"

"Minimum wage."

"I'm worth more than that. Computer skills command a high price on the market."

His smile held a cutting edge. "Then I suggest you take your skills and ply them elsewhere." He unlocked the truck and opened the door.

She climbed inside, leaping up the high step quickly.

"I've always been attracted to long-legged women," he remarked, then slammed the door.

He went around to his side, climbed in and cranked

up the engine, turning the air conditioner on full-blast. She studied him, not sure how to take his remark.

"Yeah, it bothers me, too," he said, looking her over when he stopped at a traffic signal.

"What?"

"The hunger. You feel it, too."

"Watch it. I might throw myself on you in a fit of uncontrollable passion right here in broad daylight."

He raised one thick dark eyebrow at her barb. "Right. I forgot I'm a rich rancher now. I have to be on the lookout for predatory women."

"Huh. You'd have to come with a whole mountain of gold for me to take you on."

"That wasn't the way you were acting Sunday night."

"A gentleman wouldn't have brought that up."

"Don't confuse me with your city lovers," he advised on a harsher note.

"My city—" She burst into laughter. "I'm not the sex kitten you seem to imagine, Mr. Rich Rancher. From my personal experience, which is quite limited, I think it's an overrated commodity."

She clamped her teeth into her lip. That was admitting too much. "I can't believe I said what I just said," she muttered. "You bring out the worst in me."

"Maybe it was lurking in the background all the time." His smile tipped one side of his mouth, taking the sting out of his observation. "I think we bring out something in each other, but it isn't necessarily the worst. Maybe it would be the best."

Chills, like a fever, rushed through her. "What?" she asked, not sure she should ask.

"Whatever," he drawled.

"It's odd to have this kind of give-and-take with a man. I've never found innuendo…interesting in the past." Her pause to find the right word resulted in a tepid description. Actually she found the verbal sparring with him exciting and baffling and utterly fascinating. It was so tempting it had to be sinful.

He pulled into a parking place on the main street of the town. "The Hip Hop has the best lunch in these parts. Is it okay with you?"

She agreed it was. They went into the busy little café and got the last table.

Cade turned his attention to the special listed on the chalkboard. He ordered as soon as the waitress came over. She seconded it, then studied him across the table.

She'd caught glimpses of him around the ranch the past couple of days, each time with his grandfather or his new half brother or cousin.

"It must have been difficult," she mused out loud, "to suddenly find yourself with a whole new family, your past entirely different from what you thought you knew. Like having to rediscover yourself and who you are."

"I know who I am. I'm still the same person."

"Not really. You have money now. You said yourself you'll have to become more wary of women who want you for the Kincaid name—"

"My name is Redstone. That's what it's going to stay."

Before she could reply, a woman with improbable red hair and earrings the size of saucers came in, spotted them and headed for the table.

"You're one of the new Kincaid grandsons, aren't you?" the woman said, pulling out a chair and sitting down. "Mind if I join you? The place is full today."

"Lily Mae Wheeler, isn't it?" Cade inquired.

Leanne noticed the woman didn't catch the irony in his voice or that he hadn't answered either of her questions.

"Yes. And this is..." The woman looked Leanne over, her eyes, shadowed heavily in blue and outlined in black, sparkling with interest.

"Leanne," she said, deliberately not giving a last name.

"Leanne," Lily Mae mused. "Ah. Rand Harding's sister. Hasn't he gone to your wedding?"

Leanne's mouth dropped open.

"They had to postpone it due to unforeseen circumstances," Cade supplied smoothly. "Leanne is helping us out at the ranch for a while."

Lily Mae lost interest. "What do you think about Jordan Baxter's claim on the ranch? Is it going to hold up the sale, do you think?"

Couldn't the woman see Cade didn't like being questioned? He shrugged while his eyes grew frosty.

"A lot of people think he's being cheated out of his rightful inheritance. Are all the brothers still at the ranch?" the nosy woman asked without a pause.

Cade settled back in his chair in a deceptively relaxed pose. "Only Trent and his wife."

Lily Mae leaned forward confidentially after a quick look around as if to make sure no one was listening. "Now there was a whirlwind marriage," she said with a sly smile. "And none too soon. The bride is four or five months along, isn't she?"

"Why don't you ask her?" Cade suggested. "Here, I'll write the number down. You can call her yourself and get all the details."

At the blank look on the older woman's face, Leanne spluttered into her tea glass. She tried to cover the laughter with a cough and choked.

Cade pounded her on the back, his eyes cynically amused.

Their guest was unfazed. "What happened to postpone your wedding? I hope it was nothing serious."

"A change of heart," Leanne said honestly. "I decided I needed more time to think things through."

Lily Mae nodded sympathetically, but Leanne didn't add anything. The older woman glanced pointedly at Cade. "A woman needs to make sure she chooses wisely." She laid a hand over her heart. "It hurts to lose the love of your life. I'm a widow myself."

"And divorced two or three times," Cade muttered in an aside. "Drove 'em all away with her chatter."

Leanne kept a straight face with an effort.

Their food arrived, and they fell silent as the waitress dispensed rolls and butter and refilled their glasses. Lily Mae quickly ordered, then watched the young waitress as she headed for the kitchen.

"That new girl looks familiar. Reminds me of someone I've seen before." She was silent for a minute as she mulled it over.

Leanne was sure the woman would come up with a name and recount the person's entire history. But the Kincaid ranch was her major item at the present, and she returned to that subject.

"I'm surprised about Jordan Baxter myself. Filing

that lawsuit and all,'' she confided. "He seems like a nice young man. Not like that Lexine Baxter.'' Lily Mae shook her head.

Cade narrowed his eyes but said nothing.

Leanne saw the name meant nothing to him. "Lexine Baxter used to live on the ranch next to the Kincaids',''" she explained. "Her father sold out to Jeremiah Kincaid years ago. She left town, then came back under an assumed name.'' She remembered the gruesome details because of Rand being at the ranch and in the midst of all the murders. She and Daisy had worried about him.

Lily Mae continued the story. "Lexine married poor Dugin Kincaid, then murdered him. And that wasn't the first. She killed her former partner, cool as you please, just minutes before her wedding. Dugin wasn't the last, either. She did in old Jeremiah, too. Of course, he probably deserved it. He didn't exactly live a saintly life, if you know what I mean.''

"I'm sure we do,'' Cade drawled.

"Lexine's in prison now. She's serving life.''

The waitress brought Lily Mae's lunch special. Again she stared at the girl, causing her to become flustered and nearly drop the platter.

"What's your name, honey?'' Lily Mae asked.

The waitress flushed and backed up a step. She glanced around as if looking for an escape hatch. "Emma. Emma Stover.''

"You got kinfolk around here?''

"No. Excuse me.'' The girl rushed off.

"She sure looks familiar.'' Lily Mae picked up a fork. "Now where was I? Oh, yes. Lexine Baxter. She may as well forget parole. The Kincaids carry too

much weight in this state for any parole board to set
her free. I thought the Kincaid troubles would be over
with her out of the way and not having any children,
other than poor Rafe Rawlings, the waif she aban-
doned in the woods.''

''He's the sheriff now, isn't he?'' Leanne asked,
curious in spite of her reservations about encouraging
the woman.

''Yes, he was promoted when Judd Hensley retired
and moved his family out to some ranch in the back
of beyond. I can't, for the life of me, understand why
people want to move so far from town and other people.''

Cade's dark eyes met Leanne's. *Should we give her
a clue?* his gaze seemed to ask. She gurgled in her
tea again. A tiny smile cracked his inscrutable face.

''The newspapers labeled Rafe 'Wolf Boy' when
he was found, a toddler all by himself in an aban-
doned cabin. Can you imagine doing that to your own
flesh and blood?''

''No,'' Cade said with unexpected firmness.

Leanne knew he would never abandon his
child…or the mother of that child. He would be faithful to the end if he ever married.

A black cloud descended over her spirits. She had
made such a mess of her life. She didn't even know
where to begin in order to start over.

''But here's more trouble for the Kincaids and
caused by a Baxter again,'' Lily Mae finished her
thought.

''Ready to go?'' Cade asked Leanne as soon as she
polished off the last bite.

She nodded. He paid the bill for all of them and

guided her out of the café without satisfying the gossipy woman's curiosity about them or his reactions to the pending Baxter-Kincaid lawsuit.

On the road to the ranch, she studied his stern features and wondered about his life and the woman who'd left him at the altar.

"A person has to let the past go," she said suddenly, not sure what she was trying to say or why she felt compelled to say it. "Everyone, including this Jordan Baxter guy, has to move on at some point in life."

"Thank you for those words of wisdom," Cade said with a great deal of mock solemnity as he turned onto the sparsely gravelled drive of the ranch.

"You're welcome," she replied cheerfully in spite of his sarcasm. "Did you love her very much—the woman who let you get away?"

The forbidding scowl returned.

She wasn't intimidated. "You must have, to want to marry her."

"Maybe I wanted her for her money or property."

Leanne shook her head. "You would only marry because of a great love." She sighed and thought the woman who had let him go had been very foolish.

He parked the pickup near the stable and turned to her. "Your head is just full of romantic fantasies, isn't it?"

"No."

"Yes," he contradicted. "No wonder you walked out on your bridegroom. No man can live up to a dream. Grow up, little girl. Life isn't a fairy tale. Come on. We have work to do."

When he got out of the truck, she trailed after him.

"I know that. Do you think I should have gone through the ceremony even though I'd had doubts for some time? Rand and Bill thought I was just having bridal jitters. I don't know. Marriage seems like a big step."

Cade stopped with one foot on the porch. "It is. If you really were unsure, then you did the best thing. You would have both ended up miserable. If there were children involved by the time you called it quits, it would affect more than just two lives. Children need a stable home."

She stayed close as he led the way into the house by a side door and into a bedroom. She stared around in surprise.

"Don't look so shocked. I didn't bring you here for a seduction," he remarked dryly. "My office is through here."

Recovering, she grinned and wrinkled her nose at him. "Oh, heck, just when I began to get my hopes up."

"Trouble," he muttered, flicking on the computer. "I knew it. You're gonna be nothing but trouble."

Lexine Baxter walked into the reception room and glanced around. She'd had to sweet talk the warden into letting her use a private meeting room instead of talking to her newly rediscovered daughter through a phone and inch-thick Plexiglas sheeting.

She quickly sized up the young woman who stood by the barred window looking ill at ease. She was pleased to see how pretty the girl was, even if she was rather thin.

Audra had platinum blond hair, styled in a short,

blunt cut. Her makeup was severe in a dramatic way—eyes outlined in black, prominent cheekbones emphasized with a slash of blush, full lips colored in dark red. The effect was surprisingly attractive.

But, of course, she took after her mother. Lexine had kept up her appearance no matter how restrictive and boring prison life was. She didn't plan on staying here forever.

"Audra," she said with a catch in her voice. Tears, real ones, filled her eyes. This was her possible ticket out of this dump. She held her arms out. "To think we're finally meeting. My own sweet baby—"

She broke off and dabbed at her eyes when her daughter didn't rush to her. She would have to be careful and not spook the kid.

"I'm sorry. I thought I was prepared, but seeing you…" She wiped her eyes again and patted a chair at right angles to the small sofa. "Please, sit down and tell me all about your life. Were you happy growing up?"

For the next hour she listened as her daughter told of her adoptive parents. Since Andrew Westwood had been Lexine's lover and was the real father of her twins, she knew all about Felicia and Andrew and the comfortable life Audra had shared with them. It was only after Andrew died that Felicia's shyster lawyer had gone through Audra's inheritance. Money that Lexine had been counting on.

None of them knew about Emma, though, the twin sister who was Lexine's ace in the hole, so to speak. The girl was still her legal child. A couple named Stover had tried to adopt Emma, but Lexine hadn't agreed. One never knew what the future would bring...and who would be needed.

"What about you?" Audra finally asked, winding down her boring tale. "Do you need anything?"

Lexine proceeded carefully. "Just seeing you is enough, knowing that you're alive and well. I just wish I could be with you...outside." Again she was pleased at the hitch in her voice.

Audra looked down, embarrassed.

Lexine laid a gentle hand on the girl's arm. Audra tensed and shifted away. Lexine was unperturbed. The fact that Audra had contacted her after receiving Lexine's pleading letter to hear from her daughter proved the younger woman's interest. All Lexine had to do was reel the nervous girl in slowly and carefully. She began her planned recital of ill-use by the Kincaid family.

"It was those heinous Kincaids that did this to us. They have been a thorn in the side of the Baxter family for generations. I was forced to leave because of Jeremiah Kincaid, the lecherous old man. He...was always after me. If I'd stayed, I think he would have raped me."

"Oh, no," Audra whispered.

"Yes. My family had lost everything to the Kincaids. The ranch was gone, my parents, everything. I left before I was trapped. Everyone is afraid of the powerful Kincaids, you see. They have a hand in everything in the state."

"They are influential."

"I didn't kill Jeremiah." Lexine touched her daughter's arm again. This time the girl didn't pull away. Lexine patted her arm gently and removed her hand. "I did kill my former partner. He showed up at the wedding and threatened to tell Jeremiah and Dugin who I really was. I'd come back to Whitehorn as Mary Jo Plummer and taken a job as a children's librarian. Jeremiah would never have let his only living son marry Lexine Baxter. He called me trash one time." She broke off as if overcome with emotion.

"Why didn't he and Dugin recognize you?" Audra asked.

Lexine sighed. "I'd had plastic surgery due to an accident."

Actually she'd been beaten by the man she was with at the time, but there was no need to go into specific details.

"When the surgeon rebuilt my face, I looked different," she continued. "No one in Whitehorn knew me when I returned." She touched Audra's arm again, then withdrew. "Your father was very kind to a frightened, lonely girl during those early days when I first went out on my own. That's why you were conceived."

"Oh. I'd wondered—"

Quickly, before they got sidetracked in ancient history, Lexine went on. "When my former partner showed up at the wedding, it was my worst nightmare come true. He threatened to expose my real identity to Dugin and his father. He said he would kill me if I didn't give him money after the marriage. We struggled with a gun and he— It was an accident, I swear it. I only wanted him to go away."

"Why would you marry Dugin when his father was still around?"

"I thought I'd be safe from Jeremiah." Lexine

lowered her voice. "I've never told anyone this, but I think Jeremiah arranged Dugin's death in order to get to me. But there's no way I can prove it."

"Surely with lawyers and a review of the evidence—"

Lexine shook her head. "That costs money. They took everything away from me, Dugin's legal wife, and gave it to one of Jeremiah's bastards, Jenny McCallum."

"I don't have any money," Audra said quickly.

Lexine studied her daughter. The girl was sympathetic. A little show of affection, and she could be easily manipulated. Lexine figured Felicia hadn't been overly loving to her adopted child. And children always loved their mother. It was a bond she was depending on.

"There's a sapphire mine," she said slowly, as if just remembering it. "It's on Baxter land. If we could find it, that would supply enough money for everything. I could be free again. We could be together and have a chance to get to know each other. There would be money for travel and clothes, a nice house, all the things I could never give you...and which you deserve."

Audra's eyes filled with tears. "It's been so awful these last few years. Mother was always demanding, but she's worse now. She thinks I should support her when she's the one who lost all our money."

"If we could find the sapphire mine, that would solve everything, wouldn't it?"

"Yes, but how can we? I mean, you're...here, and I don't know where it is."

"I don't know, either, not exactly, but I have a

pretty good idea. The old mining area isn't that large. A smart person could find it if she searched in a pattern, making sure to cover it all. The state has these topography maps a person can order. I've studied them closely and could show you the areas to search."

Lexine waited with enforced patience as her daughter thought it through.

"Do you think I could find it?" she finally asked.

"I think so. I'll get the maps and show you how to search. Together, we could do it. Or maybe it sounds like too much work to you. Maybe you're not interested in helping your real mother or recovering your fortune."

"Oh, I am. I want to help. The Kincaids should be brought to justice so you can be free."

"Oh, my darling girl," Lexine said on a sob. "I can't tell you how much this means to me. I didn't dare dream you would help after I had to give you up. It tore my heart out…" She covered her face with her hands.

Audra moved over to the sofa. She tentatively hugged Lexine. "Don't cry. It'll work out. I promise."

"Thank you, darling. I can't tell you what this means to me." Lexine unfastened a necklace hidden under her prison garb. "I don't have much in this world, but this locket is a keepsake. From my mother…your grandmother. She was a wonderful, loving person. I want you to have it as a remembrance of your true heritage. The Baxters of Whitehorn were once as powerful as the Kincaids."

Lexine put the necklace around Audra's throat and

accepted her thanks. Then she held the girl close while they both wept. Later she got permission to get the maps from her cell. Together she and her daughter planned the future, down to the tiniest detail. It was all going to be wonderful.

And revenge was going to be sweet.

Five

Leanne tracked the thunder with one part of her mind while she worked at the computer. She would have to turn the machine off if the storm moved into the valley.

Thunderstorms made her nervous for another reason. Her parents had died in a flash flood. Not far from their home, returning from a trip to town, her father had crossed a low spot in the road. The water hadn't looked deep, but it had caused the car to stall. Before he could get the vehicle started again, a ten-foot wall of water had crashed down on the car, sending it tumbling like a log along the ravine.

A high school senior, she'd been devastated by the loss. Rand and Daisy had put their own grief aside and been there for her. So had Bill. It had been a time of closeness for the four of them.

With Rand back at the ranch in Whitehorn, Bill had taken over his role, checking on her at the community college where she'd honed her secretarial and computer skills before taking a full-time job.

A clap of thunder startled her out of the past and into the present. She saved the file and turned the computer off.

Going to the window, she watched the wind kick up dust devils along the gravel road. Huge thunderheads roiled dark and ominous over the Crazies to the west while smaller clouds, blown by the wind, scudded over the ranch.

The remuda stirred restlessly. An unusual number of horses were at the ranch's main quarters due to the auction coming up at the end of the month. She'd seen the replies from other ranchers. They'd have a fair crowd for the sale.

In the three days she'd worked in the efficient office next to Cade's bedroom, she'd learned a lot about the ranch.

Garrett Kincaid, Cade's grandfather, seemed to like her. He didn't question her presence, although his eyes seemed to find something amusing when he'd observed her and Cade at lunch yesterday.

Trent and Gina seemed nice, too, although she avoided them as much as possible. Being on the run, so to speak, made her leery of Gina, who was, after all, a private investigator. She feared the woman might feel compelled to report her to her brother.

Glancing at the calendar, she realized her respite was running out. She'd been at the ranch a week. Rand and Suzanne, along with the kids, were due home in another week.

One week. Then she would have to decide what to do. She couldn't go back to her old job and she certainly wasn't going to work with Bill at the insurance agency.

With her parents gone, her childhood home had ceased to be. She and Rand and Daisy had split what inheritance there was after the ranch was sold and the bills were paid.

It came to her that she really and truly belonged no place in the world.

Her dream of a ranch of her own had been foolish. It took a ton of money and a lot of luck. An iffy proposition in the best of times. Farmers and ranchers often lived during the worst of times.

Drought. Flood. Insects. Disease. Life could be one disaster after another. Even without land to care for, hers certainly seemed to fit the pattern.

She tried to smile, but couldn't summon the effort. Going back to work, she began filing a stack of papers that Cade had sorted the afternoon before. She'd told him that ninety percent of all filed papers were never looked at again. He'd told her she could throw them away three years from now.

As if she'd be around.

The dark restlessness of the storm invaded her soul. She glanced out the window again. The nearest paddock was filled with horses to be sold. They milled in a circle along the fence line.

Another crack of thunder exploded directly over the house. Before she could blink, a bolt of lightning hit, formed a ball, and ran along the wires between the main house and the bunkhouse. Halfway, with a sound like a cannon exploding, it arced down to a hay rake left propped against the paddock fence.

To her amazement, the fence shimmered with a magical glow along one side before the light died out.

The horses trapped within the paddock screamed in terror. Two dropped to the ground. The rest fled, going right through the far fence, across the pasture where cattle huddled against the storm, and disappearing into the trees and rolling foothills of the open range where the ranch joined the reservation.

"The horses are out," Leanne yelled, running down the hallway toward the family room where Garrett read and napped in the afternoons. Cade sometimes went there and chatted with the older man about the ranch plans.

Gina came out of the bedroom she shared with Trent. "What?"

"Lightning hit the paddock. The horses are out."

"Can we round them up?"

Leanne shook her head. "They've lit out for the high ground. It'll take a couple of days of hard work to get them back down."

"What's happened?" Garrett asked, coming into the hall.

Leanne explained. "I'm heading for the bunkhouse to see who's available. And to find Cade."

She rushed across the quadrangle. No one was in except Cookie. "Cade was just in for coffee. He's working in the arena," he told her.

She headed for the large building that looked like an airplane hangar. That was where the auction would take place. Provided they had any horses to sell. She saw him come out and go into the stable. She changed directions.

"The horses are out," she called, entering the dim interior that smelled of horses and leather.

"I know," he replied without looking up from saddling the Appaloosa.

"Are any of the men close enough to help?"

"No."

"Which horse should I use?"

He looked at her. "You know how to handle a skittish herd?"

"Of course." She looked at the stock horses in a couple of stalls. "The big gelding looks rested."

"Pick a saddle," Cade said, tacitly agreeing to let her help. "I'm heading out."

He led the stallion outside. A second later she heard the hoof beats as the animal sped away toward the hills. She hurried to join him. They really needed three people to control a spooky herd.

She spotted Cade up ahead and rode to his left. "Up in the pine trees over this ridge," she called to him. "I'll take this side."

He nodded and angled to the right as they went over the rise and into the dip where the trees grew thickly. The land rose sharply from that point.

She came across the first band of the missing one hundred horses as soon as she entered the trees. Using a rope, she started them moving back to the other side of the ridge where the pasture started.

Another rider joined her, riding point while she drove the group from the rear. They circled them up and left them in the pasture.

"Thanks, Mr. Kincaid," she called.

"Garrett," he corrected. His grin was cheerful. "Lead the way."

She headed over the rise again. For the rest of the afternoon, the three of them herded groups of twos, threes, sometimes ten or twelve, horses to the pasture. The thunder growled, but the rain held off. They worked until nearly dark.

"Let's head 'em in," Cade called.

Again Garrett rode point while Cade took the right

side and she took the left back position. They started the herd across the pasture toward the paddock.

Every once in a while a recalcitrant mare and her group tried to make a break for the hills again, but she quickly brought them back in line. An hour later they had half the horses back in the paddock. Garrett volunteered to take care of their mounts while she and Cade repaired the fence.

The rain came before they finished. Holding the barbed wire in place as he twisted the strands together and tightened them, she heard the hard patter before the first drops hit.

"Rain," she said.

He gave a grunt of acknowledgment and continued. The heavens opened up, and they were soon drenched. Neither had a coat. Luckily the rain didn't combine with sleet and hail as it had last week. They finished up as the last of the twilight faded into total darkness.

"Go get a warm shower," Cade advised.

"Right. You, too."

"Yeah. Leanne?"

"Yes?" She waited, water running off her hat and down her back, her heart kicking into a fast trot.

"Thanks for your help."

"It was fun."

His teeth flashed white in the near dark. "Fun," he repeated with sardonic amusement. "I must have missed that part of the adventure."

"Nah. You were right in the thick of it." With a laugh and a shiver as another sweep of rain surged over them, she ran for the bunkhouse and that hot shower.

Minutes later, standing under the warm spray, she thought of him in his room, doing the same. Her breath stuck in her throat as she imagined sharing a shower with him.

She closed her eyes in despair. What was wrong with her? To…to *lust* after a man she'd known for a week… This wasn't like her. She'd never been man crazy like some of her friends. Yet she wanted Cade with a bone-deep need that unnerved and baffled her.

Why?

What drove her restless spirit to yearn for this man—a man she barely knew?

She sighed. Or was it herself she no longer knew?

Leanne breathed deeply of the crisp morning air. Dawn came early in midsummer, and she'd gotten up at first light. She'd already peeled the day's quota of potatoes and stored them, covered with water so they wouldn't turn dark, in the fridge. Cookie had been grumpily amazed when he'd walked in and found her busily at work.

A movement from the main house caught her eye. Before she was even fully conscious of who it was, her body was already reacting—heart thumping, chest tight, skin tingling.

It was Cade.

She joined him before he reached the stable.

He paused and glared at her. She smiled brightly, although her spirits drooped a bit. She didn't need a crystal ball to know he wasn't pleased to see her.

"What are you so cheery about?" he asked.

"The morning," she replied. "It's my favorite time

of the day. Everything is new, as if it was reborn during the night.''

''Huh.'' He strode on.

She followed and without a word, saddled a sweet mare with pinto markings. Cade chose a piebald gelding whose temper seemed to match his. The gelding tried to bite him twice while he saddled up. Leanne hid a grin.

''We'll be out all day,'' he said outside the stable before they mounted up. ''Did you bring food and water?''

She held up a canvas bag.

He grunted again.

She tied the lunch behind her saddle and mounted up when he did. They headed across the field toward the trees.

Jimmy brought fresh coffee and donuts out to them at nine o'clock, then helped them bring in the horses they'd found.

''Thanks, Jimmy. That was very thoughtful of you,'' Leanne said warmly when he left to return to his job of moving cattle to another pasture. ''And just in time. I was running on empty.''

After he rode off, Cade cast a sour glance her way. ''Ease off on the kid. Any more praise from you and his face would have split from grinning.''

''Jimmy's nice. And cheerful. A person would have to use a chisel to get a smile on that rock face of yours.''

That set him back for a second before he growled it was time to get back to work. He rode off.

Leanne had to admit she was glad when he signaled they should stop to rest the horses at noon. ''Oh-h,'' she groaned, plopping down on a rock and using a boulder as a backrest. "I'm not used to a full day in the saddle anymore."

"Were you ever?"

She ate and watched his quick, sure movements as he retrieved his lunch, hung his hat on the saddlehorn and chose a place to sit, then ate a sandwich piled high with ham and cheese.

He glanced around at her, a question in his eyes.

"I'm sorry. What did you say?" she said, unable to recall the topic of conversation.

"I asked if you were ever used to a full day's work in the saddle."

"Like most ranch kids, I grew up on a horse. I always thought I'd live on a ranch. When my parents died and we lost our place, it was as if I'd been yanked out by my roots. Rand and Daisy were gone, but I was still at home. The world didn't make sense anymore."

"Poor little orphan," he mocked, but there was gentleness in the tone, too.

"I knew I couldn't afford another ranch on my own, but I thought, when I found the right person, we would do it together."

"Instead your fiancé bought a house in the country club set?" Cade questioned.

She nodded. "He said it would be good for the insurance business, that we would make more money if we had a wealthy clientele." She sighed and shook her head. "Maybe I was wrong to accuse him of lying to me and using my money for his own selfish plans. Maybe I am being foolish and headstrong as he said. Rand thought so."

Guiltily she thought of her brother. And her sister. Rand would be angry with her while Daisy would be worried at her disappearance. They had watched over her for years. Leanne loved them more than she had ever loved Bill.

"A person has to follow his or her own dream," Cade said in a deeper, quieter tone. "No one can force you to accept another's as yours. It isn't right of them to try to make you."

"Then you think I was right to walk out?"

His expression changed to sardonic as he shrugged. "I didn't say that. But a person ought to be sure before committing to a long-term arrangement."

She nodded, feeling the tiniest bit vindicated in her decision to not go through with the marriage, although she didn't harbor any illusions that Cade thought much of her in any way, form or fashion.

The day had warmed considerably since dawn. She'd already removed her denim jacket. Now she laid her hat aside and unbuttoned the blue work shirt, then rolled the sleeves back on her arms.

Perspiration stained the T-shirt she wore underneath to a deeper shade of blue from the neckline to a vee disappearing into the valley between her breasts where her bra soaked up the rest of the moisture. She wiped her forehead on her sleeve and blew a wisp of hair out of her eyes.

Closing her eyes and leaning her head against the boulder, she murmured, "Doesn't it feel good to sit here in the shade with nothing but the sound of the wind and a few sleepy calls from blue jays to keep us company?"

He didn't answer.

She opened her eyes. His gaze was on her, moving slowly from point to point. Her mouth. Her throat. The damp vee of her T-shirt.

Without taking his eyes from her, he crumpled the bag of corn chips in his fist, then tossed it aside. She saw his chest rise and fall in a sharply drawn and released breath.

"Cade?"

She heard the uncertainty in her voice. And the yearning. So did he.

He looked into her eyes, his face grim. The intensity of his hunger seared through her, shocking her. Flames licked at her insides, destroying whatever sense of survival resided there.

His gaze still locked with hers, he crossed the few feet that separated them and settled beside her.

The moment lengthened, grew into an agony of longing, before he touched her. Raking his fingers into her hair, he pressed them against her scalp.

She didn't hesitate, but moved forward, lifting her face. She clasped her arms around his neck.

In an instant their lips met and merged into a fiery kiss of passionate need. He slanted his mouth across hers, first one way, then the other. He explored her mouth, sucked on her tongue, stroked the inside of her lips.

Her heart went wild.

He crushed her closer, then lifted her and sat her across his lap, taking her place against the boulder.

"What is it with you?" he murmured at one point. "What is it about you that's so damn hard to resist?"

"I don't know." She kissed him all over his jaw, his neck, down to his shirt. "What is it about you?"

"Wait." He stripped the shirt off, revealing deeply tanned skin with a diamond of wiry hair. His hands went to her shirt and he waited.

When she sat up straight, he pushed the material past her shoulders, then slipped it down her arms and flung it on top of his.

"Take the other off," he said, his voice husky.

Taking hold of the hem of the T-shirt, she raised it over her head and dropped it to the ground.

He groaned and pulled her to him, planting kisses over her burning flesh from her throat to her bra. She felt the hooks release, then the material being pushed aside.

"You're exactly as I've remembered every night in my dreams. Perfect. Succulent."

He pressed her gently back against his arm, then dipped his head and touched her breast. She held her breath.

With the gentlest of caresses, he brushed his lips over the very tip, then smiled at her response. His gaze was so hot on her, she wondered why she hadn't simply burst into flames at the first glance.

With trembling fingers she touched his chest, running her hand over the hard muscles. With her other hand, she explored his back, then ran her fingers through his dark, silky hair.

"You make me feel weak," she whispered, a protest as sense slipped farther and farther away.

"That isn't half of what touching you does to me," he told her, irony and laughter in the words.

"What? Tell me."

"You know."

She did. The evidence of his desire pressed against

her hip, adding to the intense awareness between them. With a keening sound deep in her throat, she turned her face into his neck. Warmth spread from him to her, from her to him, wrapping them in a special lover's cocoon of passion that excluded the rest of the world.

"It scares me, to want this much," she explained as he stroked her back from neck to waist. "I've never felt this…this need. It's like a fire in the blood."

"It's that," he agreed, nuzzling her hair.

He laid a hand on her side, then smoothed it upward until his thumb brushed the side of her breast. After a bit, he moved again, this time sliding his hand between them. She shifted so he could reach her easily. He cupped her breast in his strong, exquisitely gentle hand.

She sighed against his throat and let the heat consume her. She didn't care about anything but this man and this moment. Some part of her worried about that.

But only for a second.

"Give me your mouth again. You make me ache, and only you can stop it."

Strange, but she knew exactly what he meant. When he laid her on their shirts, she went willingly. His chest pressed against hers as he stretched out beside her, his thigh nestled between hers. She gazed into his eyes and saw the fire in his.

There was more. Things she couldn't read—emotion drawn from the past that he guarded himself against, questions that neither of them could answer. She didn't understand, but she sensed he was vulnerable at this moment. And so was she. "None of this makes any sense," she whispered.

"I know."

He claimed her mouth again. The kiss went deep, and deeper still, making her heart jumpy, its beats erratic and somewhat frightening.

He kissed her breasts and tongued her nipples. She rubbed his until they contracted into hard beads like her own. The way he'd done to hers, she set out to explore his body. The pounding pulse point at his neck, the rich hardness of his chest. But when she slipped a hand beneath the waistband of his jeans, he stopped her.

"We're not going that far. I don't have protection with me. I didn't think I'd need it on a roundup."

She felt his chuckle as well as heard it. She managed a smile, although she felt heavy, languid, and yet incredibly tense, every nerve humming with energy.

"I know. I never thought to find this when I came here. Kiss me again, Cade."

He shook his head. "I want you. But another minute or two and we'll both forget the lessons of the past. The consequences might be more than we want to pay."

"What consequences?" She shivered as he traced lazy circles over her body, making her breasts ache for more of his wonderful caresses.

"We could make a baby."

His eyes went darker as he gazed moodily down at her. She exhaled shakily. The thought didn't frighten her, though she knew it should.

He rested his head against hers. "If we made love,

we'd complicate a situation that's already too entangled.''

It seemed to Leanne that this was the only simple thing in her life—this attraction that had no right to be, no cause to exist. Neither of them had asked for it.

Slowly the tension drained out of his body. After a while she realized he was asleep. An act of trust. She yawned and snuggled closer. With him, she felt safe, too.

It seemed only a minute later that she felt his touch on her shoulder. "Come on. It's time to get back to work.''

She roused and stretched, then realized she was bare up top. Instinctively crossing one arm over her breasts, she reached for a covering. He beat her to it. He handed her the bra, then the T-shirt, and waited until she had them on before holding her work shirt as she slipped her arms into it.

''That's odd. I slept better for an hour on the hard ground than in my bed this past week.'' He cocked a dark eyebrow. ''Must be the fresh air.''

She frowned at him, not sure what she should be feeling just now. ''I don't understand this, Cade.'' She gestured toward the ground where they had lain. ''We can't...I can't become involved with you. I was supposed to be in love with another man only a week ago.''

His expression became guarded. ''A few hot kisses didn't commit either of us to anything.''

''Of course not,'' she agreed at once. ''I know it doesn't, but I want to be up-front with you. I don't want an affair—''

"You think I do?" He pulled on his shirt and went to where the horses grazed on the lush mountain grass. He tightened the girth on the gelding, grabbed the reins and swung up. "Come on, Annie, we got work to do."

"Annie?" she questioned as she did the same.

"As in 'Little Orphan'," he explained.

She grimaced at his back as they headed deeper into the back country to rout out the last of the missing horses. She felt orphaned as she struggled with her conscience about wanting Cade and hurting Bill and her family. She worried about her morals that she could so quickly go from one man—who hadn't stirred much of anything in her but should have—to another—who stirred her to her depths and shouldn't.

"Cade," she said as they rode along the trail, "I'm worried about my steadfastness. What kind of person am I?"

"Everything I don't need in my life." He turned to face her. "Passionate. Impulsive. Headstrong."

"Sorry I asked," she said, stung by the criticism.

"You're also good with the horses. You can help me with them, but only if you get the computer set up first."

She brightened at the thought. Maybe she could live here at the ranch. She'd become indispensable to Cade and he would want her to stay. Maybe things would work out....

Six

"We buried the two horses we lost due to the lightning hit, but we've recovered the rest—every one of 'em," Cade reported to Garrett the following day at lunch. "Thanks to your help."

"And Leanne's," the older man observed. "She's a good worker, isn't she?"

Cade hesitated only a moment. "Seems to be."

"Who's this?" Collin Kincaid, the one legitimate son and heir to the Elk Springs ranch, asked.

"Harding's sister."

When he added nothing further, Trent spoke up. "She didn't get married as planned, but came here to think things over for a while."

Collin looked puzzled. "She's working here?"

"Yes," Cade snapped, aware of the amused glance between Trent and Gina. "She's setting up the breeding program on the computer. She's also helping the cook over at the bunkhouse. I figured she ought to earn her keep while waiting for her brother to return from vacation."

"I see. I think," Collin added drolly. He turned to his grandfather. "What's the situation with the ranch?"

Garrett frowned. "Baxter has filed an injunction. He's claiming first rights at buying, as his uncle promised. He's also saying he's offered more and that the trustees are cheating Jenny McCallum out of her inheritance by selling for a lesser amount.''

"Your offer is market price. Baxter made a pre-emptive bid, but he can't raise that kind of money," Trent mentioned. "Gina checked his resources."

"Only those of public record," she quickly stated. "I didn't go into his personal accounts."

"I feel sorry for him," Garrett said suddenly. "It's tough to give up a dream. He thought the Baxter place would be his someday." He turned to Cade. "I understand the Appaloosa mare you bought will be foaling any day."

"She's showing all the signs. I've brought her into the stable for the birthing. It's her first, so I'd like to be on hand if she needs help."

"Good. Wayne reports the calf count is up this year, so the ranch should break even or even be in the black this fall for the first time in years."

Collin spoke up. "With the new cattle we're bringing in from the other place, we'll get a better beef herd within a couple of years."

Cade answered questions on the auction. "I've got a bid on the whole string from a rancher down in Texas, but one of the other ranchers asked to look at the bunch before we accept. I've decided to go ahead with the auction since we've already sent out the information." He stood. "I'm heading for the stable to check the mare."

At the stable, he heard the mare whicker, then a soft murmur. Heat flashed through his body, alerting him to who was with the animal without seeing her. He propped his arms on the stall door and watched as Leanne stroked the mare's neck. He noted the stall was clean and fresh straw was strewn on the floor. Clean rags lay close at hand in case they were needed.

"How does she look?" he asked.

Leanne jerked around. "I didn't hear you come in," she said, a blush rising to her cheeks. "She's dilated quite a bit, but the contractions aren't all that strong. I checked the position of the foal. It's fine."

His skepticism must have showed.

"I was born on a ranch. I know a thing or two."

He eased into the stall and examined the mare. The animal glanced at him with big, suffering eyes as she went into another contraction. It wasn't a long one.

"Let's walk her," he suggested. "Maybe that will speed things along."

"That's what I was thinking, too." She gave him a serious, concerned glance before clucking to the mare, who lay in the straw. "Come on, girl, let's take a walk. That will make you feel better. Yeah, that's it. Come on now." She led the horse out of the stall. "What's her name?"

"Delilah. Because she was the prettiest of all the fillies on the ranch, according to the previous owner."

She grimaced, then laughed. "I would have called her Mopsy because of the hair that keeps falling in her eyes."

They took turns walking the mare for the rest of the afternoon. By dark, Cade was getting worried.

Leanne sat on a bale of straw and wiped her face with a handkerchief dampened at the utility sink in the tack room. She looked up at Cade, a question in her eyes.

He waited out another contraction, then led the

mare into the stall. She sank into the clean straw as if too tired to stand any longer. He soaped his hands and arms and rinsed, then gently examined the horse. "Bring me that piece of rope over there," he said.

She removed the rope from a nail and handed it to him. He held it in his mouth and, giving a great heave, brought the foal's forelegs into the open. He quickly tied the rope on. Leanne moved over to help while he rinsed his hands.

Together they pulled each time the mare went into a contraction. Each time a bit more of the foal came into view. It was a slow, taxing process.

"She's tired," Cade said at one point, wiping sweat on his sleeve. "She's not helping much now."

"The foal has got to come out."

"I agree." He hooked a pulley on the stall door and threaded the rope through it. "A big pull this time."

She nodded and got into position, wrapping the rope once around her palms for a good grip.

At the next contraction, Cade moved behind her. He reached around her and grasped the rope, his big, strong hands alternating with hers. They leaned against the rope and pulled with all their might.

She felt his chest against her back, the short puffs of breath against her hair when he panted with exertion.

"Steady," he said. "Keep the pressure on."

Slowly the foal slipped into view—a nose, the eyes and ears, finally the shoulders. The mare grunted and pushed to her feet. Her sides heaved as if she'd been running.

"Rest now," Cade said in a soothing tone.

"You're doing good, girl. Once more and we'll have it."

The mare huffed, and the next contraction began. The tiny back hooves appeared, then the haunches. It was over in a rush. Leanne fell against Cade as the pressure of tugging suddenly released.

He closed his arms around her. "Watch," he said quietly.

The mare sniffed at the baby, then gave a tentative lick at its rump. The foal's head, wobbling as if it were a toy on a spring, bobbed around. The mother licked vigorously at its little face, making the head bobble more.

Leanne felt Cade's soft laugh. She laid her arms over his, her hands touching his, and rested her head against his chest. "A filly," she whispered as the foal tried to stand.

"Good."

She smiled. A ranch was one place where females were appreciated and usually desired over males. Feeling connected with life and procreation, she enjoyed the tactile sense of their bodies—their warmth, the perspiration that soaked their shirts where they touched, the camaraderie of sharing one of the elemental experiences of life.

His lips caressed the side of her neck. She tilted her head and closed her eyes as tingles arced down into the inner core of her body. She lifted one hand and stroked his cheek, the damp strands of hair at his temple.

When his hands moved upward, she instinctively thrust forward. His hands closed over her breasts. He licked the salty dampness at her throat while massaging her breasts in a sensual pattern.

Excitement swept through her. She became hot, tense, damp. Her body was ready for his.

"Cade," she whispered in painful need.

He turned her in his arms and claimed her mouth. Willingly, eagerly, she went to him. His hands slipped down her back and cupped her hips, pulling her against him. She twisted slightly, brushing back and forth, arousing him and herself with the subtle pleasure.

"Let's get out of here," he murmured.

They looked at the mare and filly once more, then left the stall.

Cade pressed her against the wall of the old stable, lifting her off her feet. She wrapped her legs around his lean hips and rocked against him.

He groaned softly, then nibbled her neck in gentle forays of passion.

"Make love to me," she demanded. "Now."

He shook his head and buried his face in her hair, which had come loose from its band as they'd worked with the mare.

"Don't you have—"

"Yes," he said hoarsely. "But we're not— You're not to tempt me beyond control."

She leaned her head against the planking and stared up at him, unable to hide her disappointment. She felt she would scream if he didn't make love to her.

"I can't stand it." She planted kisses all over his face, as much as she could reach. "I want you. I don't want to stop, not this time."

He laughed, a rough growl of need and frustration. "Do you think I do?"

"Then why...?"

"One of us has to think."

She unclasped her legs and slid down his long, lean, utterly masculine body. She laid her cheek on his chest. "Your heart is beating so fast," she murmured.

"So is yours. A fine fix we've found ourselves in, isn't it?"

The sardonic edge was back in his voice. She kissed his chest above the opening of his shirt and tasted the salt on his skin. "What do you mean?"

"I came here to meet a family I never knew I had. You came to escape yours that you know all too well." He was silent a moment. "Don't let them talk you into anything you're not sure of."

"It's hard. I know they want only the best for me. I don't want to hurt them. Or Bill."

"But you don't love him," Cade cut in, "not the way a woman should love the man she's going to marry."

She didn't answer.

His hands tightened around her waist. "Do you?"

"I don't know. I care for him. He's been a friend all my life. He says we're in love."

"But you don't share this." He moved against her, bringing a gasp of pleasure to her lips. "How could you consider marrying a man you don't want this way?"

She shook her head. "I guess I answered that when I left before the ceremony. I feel so terrible about letting everyone down." She sighed, then gazed up at him. "Kiss me some more, Cade. In your arms, I forget how awful I am."

Cade took in the weary smile, the sadness in her eyes. He held her close. For a long minute he battled an impulse to ride off into the hills with her and to hell with everyone and everything.

A strange sensation gripped his chest. He had the oddest need to protect her, not just from her family, but from her own mixed-up loyalty to them and her ex-fiancé. It wasn't something he'd experienced in his previous thirty-five years, and it confused him.

He had a feeling this woman could make him act the fool with very little effort. He remembered how it was standing in front of family and friends and telling them there would be no wedding. He wouldn't be that big a fool again for any female, no matter that she came to him like a gift from the storm, looking lost and frightened and weary beyond endurance. Her family was her problem, not his.

"It's late," he said in a growl. "We'd better go in."

Her eyes were softly pleading. He didn't think she was even aware of the need. He resisted for all of five seconds, then he bent and kissed her again, this time very slowly and very gently. The hunger trembled through her as she leaned against him.

The need was mutual. His body demanded he take her to his room and keep her there for hours and hours. Until they had drunk their fill of each other. He suppressed the images with an effort.

"Out," he ordered with a rueful smile when he lifted his mouth from hers.

He opened the stable door and walked up the road,

his arm around her shoulders. He stopped at the point where she needed to cross the road to the bunkhouse.

"Good night," she said.

He liked the slight tremor in her voice, the candid way her eyes searched his face in the faint light, the fact that she didn't act coy or falsely shy about their passion. He touched her lips with a finger, lingered to caress their softness, absorb their heat.

"Go on in," he said, and stayed in the shadows to watch until she was safely inside.

When she reached the door of the bunkhouse, she emitted a startled "Oh!"

Cade saw another shape, that of a man, materialize out of the dark. The man grabbed Leanne's wrist.

"What's your hurry, sweetheart?"

Gil. Cade frowned and moved silently across the road, sticking to the shadows. If Leanne could handle it, he wouldn't interfere. If not, then Gil had a lesson coming he wouldn't soon forget.

"Oh, hi, Gil," she said in casual surprise. "I didn't see you. The mare foaled tonight. We have the most beautiful little filly you ever saw."

Gil snorted. "I saw you in the stable. Didn't look to me like you were paying much attention to the filly."

She laughed. "I guess I got a little emotional after the birth. Poor Cade probably was shocked out of his mind when I nearly hugged him to death."

"There was more than hugging going on," Gil said in a suggestive manner.

"Well, we both got a little carried away with the moment. Luckily Cade is a gentleman." She paused and looked straight at the cowboy. "Like all the men here at the ranch, I hope. I'd hate to scream and cause a big commotion. It could be embarrassing.''

Cade started forward when Gil didn't let go of her right away. He would beat the man to a pulp.

Gil dropped her arm and laughed falsely. ''Yeah, we're all true-blue heroes.''

The door opened, spilling light onto the porch. Leanne politely held it until Gil disappeared inside. She turned and waved jauntily.

Cade relaxed. With a smile whose cause he couldn't identify, he headed for the main house and a comfortable bed. He would have chosen a bed of straw that night if it had been with her, he realized.

Leanne greeted the dawn with more than her usual worshipful attendance. A quietness had entered her soul. An introspective mood engulfed her. When she thought of Cade, her heart gave a hitch. She wasn't sure of herself or anything, but she seemed to have entered a waiting period.

She just didn't know what she was waiting for.

Going to the stable, she checked on the new mother and baby. There was food in the manger and fresh straw on the floor. Cade had already been in. Her heart lurched as she thought of him.

Shaking her head, she returned to the bunkhouse and started peeling potatoes. Cookie came in a few minutes later and gave her a mock frown.

''You're the only person I ever knew who got up just so's she could say hello to the sun.''

''I like the morning.''

He snorted and poured a cup of coffee from the huge pot that she'd already made. It was the first of many that got the cowboys through the hard days of tending a ranch.

After the breakfast dishes were clean and put away, she headed for Cade's office. Flicking on the computer, she realized they had the first birth to record in the new data program. She glanced at his bedroom door and wondered where he was. She hadn't seen him outside all morning, only the evidence that he'd taken care of the mare and foal earlier.

Around ten, Gina stopped at the hall door. "How about a break? I could use some coffee and a snack to tide me over until lunch."

Leanne nodded and saved the file she was working on. "We have a new filly who needs a name. She's Appaloosa and should have beautiful markings when she matures."

"What's her mother's and father's names?"

They discussed it on the way to the dining room. There they found Garrett, Cade and Trent. Another man was with them.

"All the grandsons will be here for the auction," Garrett was telling Cade. "Ah, the ladies," he said, breaking off the discussion when Leanne and Gina entered. "Please join us. Have you met my grandson, Collin?" he asked Leanne. "This is Leanne Harding, who's visiting and helping us out for a while."

Leanne felt awkward and self-conscious around Cade's family, as if she were there under false pretenses. Which she was, she reminded herself. No one but Cade knew that her family still didn't know where she was. In less than a week they would return. And then what?

She didn't know.

Trent served Gina in a sweet display of husbandly thoughtfulness. Leanne's eyes met Cade's.

"Good morning," he said. "Have you been to the stable?"

She nodded. "They seem to be doing well."

"I'll turn them out to pasture in a bit." He refilled his coffee cup, then held out a chair for her next to him.

Surprised and shockingly pleased at this courtesy, she sat and nibbled on a pastry that could have been a mud pie for all the notice she gave it. She couldn't get past last night and the kisses she and Cade had shared.

"Was it a difficult birth?" Gina asked.

"Well, a slow one," Cade admitted. "But there were no complications to speak of."

His eyes met Leanne's again. She felt herself blushing and bent her head over her coffee cup as if enthralled with the aroma rising on the steam. Every part of her was awash in memories of last night.

The touch of his hands as they'd roamed freely over her. The way his mouth could be gentle or demanding. The hard masculine feel of his body and the way touching him made her feel very feminine.

She lost track of the conversation and was abruptly brought back to reality by a commotion in the front hall.

"I want to see Kincaid right now. Not Wayne. I want the old man," an angry male voice said, speaking quickly and loudly.

Garrett rose. Cade, Gina, and the men stood as one and headed for the entrance. Leanne trailed after them.

Jordan Baxter stood in the foyer. He smiled in triumph when he spotted Garrett and waved a piece of paper at the Kincaid patriarch. "I found it," he declared. "The letter my uncle wrote, promising me the ranch. He gave me the right of first refusal if he had to sell. It's rightfully mine."

Collin started to speak, but Garrett touched his grandson's arm. He held out a hand for the letter.

Jordan handed it over. "It's a copy, so don't think you can destroy it. The original is with my attorney."

Garrett read the letter, then shook his head, his expression sympathetic. Gina asked to see it.

"Look at the date on this," she said to the older man. "The statute of limitations ran out long ago. It would have had to be invoked when Jeremiah Kincaid bought the Baxter ranch. It's too late now."

"You lie," Jordan accused.

Trent took a step forward. Gina stopped him by the simple expedient of leaning against him.

Baxter continued. "My attorney says otherwise. Since you won't see reason and withdraw, we'll leave it to the courts to decide."

"It doesn't have to come to that," Garrett said. "Gina is right."

"You'll see," Jordan promised. He stormed out as suddenly as he'd arrived.

Garrett shook his head sadly and gestured to the letter Gina still held. "Better add it to the file of things to be looked into. Would you fax a copy to the ranch lawyer? He'll need to see it."

She promised she would.

Cade walked out onto the front porch of the ranch house. He watched Jordan Baxter drive down the gravel road at a furious, reckless pace. Like Garrett, he felt sorry for the man. He knew how it hurt to give up a dream. Baxter hadn't given up yet, but it was only a matter of time. Cade agreed with Garrett and Gina. The man really didn't have a case.

Before Baxter drove out of sight, Cade spotted another vehicle on the ranch road. Two of them.

He watched as Rand Harding and his family arrived home. The second car, too, stopped at the foreman's house. A man climbed out and joined the others as they went inside.

He'd better warn Leanne that her family was back. She was going to have to face the music a bit earlier than she'd planned.

The surge of sympathy surprised him. He couldn't figure out how she'd gotten under his skin so fast. Neither could he fathom why he kept experiencing this need to step between her and her family and the ex-fiancé as if she needed his protection.

He checked the dining room but found only his grandfather and Collin. He went on down the hall to his office, where he found Leanne at the computer.

"Prepare yourself," he advised, keeping his tone neutral. "Rand has arrived."

"He's early," she protested. Worry leaped into her eyes, making them as dark as a mossy bank in the forest.

He shrugged. "Guess he got enough vacation." He paused. "There was a stranger with him."

She looked stricken. "A man?"

"Yeah. About your brother's age. Light brown hair. Rangy frame."

"Bill."

When she glanced at him, her face flamed, surprising and intriguing him. Her mouth looked soft. Vulnerable.

He wanted to kiss it until she trembled against him the way she'd done last night. "You were going to have to face him sooner or later anyway," he reminded her.

She gave a tiny fatalistic smile. "I'd hoped for later." She stood and smoothed down her shirt, hesitated, then buttoned the green work shirt over the T-shirt.

He liked the shirt open so he could see the rise of her breasts under the cotton T-shirt. He liked to touch her and feel the kick of her heart against his palm. He liked to cup the succulent fullness and feel the tip bead in his hand.

His body hardened so fast he nearly gasped. "You're going to be the death of me," he muttered.

Her gaze dropped down and saw his problem. Instantly she blushed and her teeth bit into her bottom lip. He was learning she did that when she was nervous or unsure of herself.

"I'd better go." Abruptly, she rushed toward the door.

Unable to stay behind, he went, too. They only got as far as the front porch before encountering a furious Rand Harding. The rejected fiancé was with him.

"You're here!" Harding exploded. "We've looked for you for the past nine days, then find you here."

"It was the one place I thought you wouldn't think of looking," she admitted.

"We didn't," Bill said. "We went everywhere

else, including the cabin where your folks used to go
when we were kids.''

"Do you realize how worried we were?'' her
brother demanded, looming over her.

She lowered her head and nodded. "I'm sorry. I
left a note—''

"Saying you were going to a friend's house,'' he
snapped. "Not exactly where you ended up.''

"Well, I didn't want you to know.''

"We truly were concerned,'' Bill broke in, stepping closer to her. "You can be so...impulsive.''

Cade watched the two men lecture Leanne, the
brother angry, the friend buttressing his words with
concern and sympathy. He heard them express *their*
worry, *their* effort at finding her. He didn't hear anyone mention her feelings or the trauma of a bride,
already dressed in her finery, running from her own
wedding.

He saw her shoulders droop and her eyes mist over
as she stoically listened to the lecture. He moved forward, close enough that she would be able to feel his
warmth there behind her. He was shocked at just how
badly he wanted to tell these two bozos to back off.
With tremendous effort he held his tongue and his
temper.

"I'm sorry,'' Leanne said, her eyes appealing to
both men to understand. "I tried to explain—''

"Look, I'm sorry about the house, darling.'' Bill
laid a hand on her shoulder and stroked her as if
soothing a nervous animal. "I wanted it to be a surprise. I didn't realize it would upset you so much.''

Cade gritted his teeth at the urge to knock the guy's
hand off Leanne. He laid his hand lightly at her waist

to let her know he was there if she needed him. She pressed against him, welcoming his touch. That pleased him.

Watching the two men crowd in on her, he understood why she had left. He sensed her love for her family and her reluctance to hurt them, including the man who was an old family friend. He wondered if she would succumb to their blandishments if they kept on long enough.

That was something he wouldn't allow.

He didn't know the whys and wherefores of the decision he'd just made, only a gut-deep knowledge that it was right. He edged in a bit closer.

Rand glanced at him, then at Leanne. "Let's go into the house, where we can relax and talk this over."

Without this outsider listening in, was what he meant.

Cade tightened his hold on Leanne while he smiled coolly at Rand and Bill. "Leanne stays with me."

Three pairs of eyes stared at him with varying expressions in their depths. Only the luminous green ones affected him, stirring something passionate and protective within him. Gazing at her brother and his friend, Cade felt anger rising in him. Without stopping to analyze it further, he said the first thing that came to mind.

"Don't you think we should tell them, darling?" he asked, smiling as he bent to murmur lover-like against Leanne's ear.

"Tell us what?" Harding demanded.

The old friend's eyes narrowed. His hands closed into fists, but at least they were off Leanne.

"Leanne and I were married a couple of days ago. My wife and I have no secrets from each other."

He felt the tremor shake all the way through her. Disbelief made comic faces on the two men as they fell back a step. His own reaction was more than a little stunned. He'd recognized the innate need to protect her, but not the lengths to which he was willing to go.

Gazing at the stunned faces of the others, including his supposed wife, his smile widened. There was something to be said for stupendous announcements.

Seven

"He's lying," Rand said, his gaze narrowing on Leanne.

To her own amazement, Leanne shook her head. She didn't know why Cade had said what he did, she didn't know why she wasn't denying it, but she didn't have time to figure it out at this moment.

"You're married to this...this guy?" Bill demanded in total disbelief, obviously failing to come up with a description for Cade allowable in polite company.

"Yes," she heard herself say. "We...we are." She felt as if she were another person, that she was watching herself and this little drama being played out from a front row seat. Another tremor raced through her.

Rand opened his mouth. Bill looked at him as if waiting for a clue on how to react. Her brother's face hardened. "You've made your bed. Now you'll have to lie in it. Don't come to me if it isn't to your liking." He stalked off.

Bill hesitated, looking from her to Cade, doubt in his eyes. "We'll talk later and maybe make some sense of all this." He followed after Rand.

A terrible heaviness descended on her. She'd disappointed her brother and hurt Bill. The supposed marriage had left them with nothing to do or say since it was presented as a done deal.

Aware of Cade standing quietly behind her, she faced him, slowly, reluctantly, almost fearfully. "Why?" was all she could manage to say.

His eyes bored into hers as if searching for the answer to her question. Finally he shrugged. "You wanted the two weeks your brother was supposed to have been gone to think things over. Now you'll have them."

"Rand knows we're lying. He only has to ask your family to find out the truth."

"My family will believe whatever I tell them."

"How're you going to explain this farce to them?" Her worry shifted to include him and the repercussions from the powerful Kincaid family.

"That we got married in a fever? That we were overcome with passion? We've been to town this past week. Who's going to say we didn't tie the knot?"

His grin was so insolent she wanted to hit him. She wanted him to be serious. She wanted… She sighed and gave up on hopeless wishes.

"Your sister-in-law for one," she reminded him. "She's a private investigator. Garrett apparently uses her for a lot of things."

"My grandfather won't question the marriage."

"I wish my brother would take my word and leave me alone," she said glumly, envisioning the coming lectures. "He means well—"

"You're a big girl now," Cade interrupted. "Take control of your own life. Without running away to do it."

She lowered her head at the criticism. "I'm not

sure I could have held out against both Rand and Bill if I'd stayed.''

Cade didn't look sympathetic.

"What now?" she asked. "You got us into this latest mess. Now get us out."

He stroked his chin as he thought. "First, we move your things from the bunkhouse to my room—"

"What?" she squeaked.

He gave her a facetious smile. "If we're supposed to be married and everyone knows it now, won't it look a bit strange if we don't share a room?"

"I hadn't thought that far ahead." She bit down hard on her bottom lip as emotion rose in her. She wasn't going to wail like a baby. She didn't even know why she felt like it. "You're right."

"Well, will miracles never cease?" he murmured. "The lady agrees for once."

Glaring at him, she headed for her room, with him walking beside her. The heat had already taken over the day, and the air shimmered over the hills around them. She wondered if hell was half as hot…or if she was already there and didn't know it.

Or maybe she did. She glanced at the tall, silent man beside her and smiled ruefully.

"What's so funny?" he asked, but in a friendlier tone than any other he'd used with her that morning.

"This has to be a classic case of 'out of the frying pan and into the fire.'"

"Yeah. In more ways than one," he agreed enigmatically.

She sighed as she entered the bunkhouse. Cookie was reading the paper and having a cup of coffee. He didn't pay any attention to them other than to relay a cursory glance.

In less than ten minutes she had her few belongings packed and ready to go. Cade picked up her canvas bag and started for the door.

"You leaving now that your brother's back?" Cookie asked, looking mildly disappointed.

"She's moving in with me," Cade answered easily. "We're married."

They left Cookie with his mouth open.

Leanne kept up with Cade's long stride until they entered his room by the verandah's side door. There, the full implications of the situation hit her. She stopped, unable to tear her gaze from the big bed that dominated the room.

"We can't do this," she said.

"What?" He put the bag on a hassock in front of an easy chair and turned leisurely to study her.

"Live a lie." She waved a hand at the bed. "Co-habit," she added for lack of a better word.

He gave her a sexy perusal. "That wasn't what you said last night."

To her chagrin, she felt her face grow hot. She didn't have to peer into a mirror to know she was beet red.

"And don't remind me about gentlemanly conduct," he added on a more irritable note. "Where you're concerned, I'm no gentleman. I want to make love with you. It's that simple."

She slumped down onto the bed, realized where she was and jumped up. "I'm not much of a lady around you, so I guess we're even."

He gave a snort of wry amusement and shook his

head. "You have a way of being totally candid that's downright disconcerting at times."

Resolute, she stared him straight in the eye. "I'm not going to sleep with you, Cade."

He raised one dark eyebrow mockingly.

"I'm not. It wouldn't be fair to Bill—"

Cade broke in with an expletive regarding the ex-fiancé.

"What kind of person would I be if I fell into bed with one man after running out on my wedding to another little more than a week ago?" She added quickly, glumly, "You don't have to answer that." She sighed, not sure what to do.

"Look," he said impatiently, "we've bought you the time you said you needed. You could have denied the lie, but you didn't. Until you do, you'll act the part of my wife. If I catch you playing around with good ol' Bill, I'll knock his teeth down his throat. And lock you in this room."

"You might try," she retorted.

He took a slow breath, released it, then walked out the door, leaving her standing there primed for battle with no one to fight with. It was the most frustrating experience of her life. No, she amended, only one of many where Cade Redstone was concerned.

Cade stood at the corral and watched the horses frolic in the sun. The fierce anger eased. In its place came a sense of calm acceptance. For whatever it was worth, he was involved right up to his neck with the runaway bride and her problems. He heaved a sigh, still not sure why he'd spoken up. Marriage. When he jumped into trouble, he did it with both feet.

Hearing footsteps, he turned defensively.

Garrett smiled and leaned beside him at the fence, his eyes on the horses. "I just heard the news."

Cade didn't bother to ask what news. Rumor spread through the grapevine faster than the speed of light. "I'm sorry we didn't tell you first," he said cautiously.

"Well, I was surprised but not overwhelmed. I saw how it was between you and the girl."

Cade was silent, thinking about those first moments in the cabin. Leanne in her bedraggled bridal outfit. In the pretty robe and gown. In his clothing.

"It was the same for me when I met your grandmother," Garrett continued. "After I saw her, no other woman would do. Looks like the same thing happened between you two."

"Sir..." Cade began, the lie heavy on his conscience. This was the one person, other than his parents, he hated to deceive. Perhaps he should tell Garrett the truth and explain why he'd felt Leanne had needed drastic action to protect her from her family.

Garrett held up a hand. "It's all right. Whatever is between you and your bride is your business. I'll say no more. Only...don't let this chance of happiness slip through your fingers. Hold on tight, son, no matter what happens or what others might say."

With this enigmatic advice, he nodded and headed back to the house, his gait displaying the bounce and energy of a much younger man. Cade stared, baffled by his grandfather's obvious satisfaction in the situation. He wondered if the old man knew they were lying and was encouraging them to hold to it.

Cade didn't know. Hell, he didn't know anything anymore.

Leanne felt speared by four pairs of eyes when she went into the dining room at lunch. Gina had stopped by the office and told her the meal was ready, her eyes sparkling with undisguised humor and interest.

"Have you met Wayne Kincaid?" Garrett asked after seating her to his right.

There was an empty chair beside her, reserved for her errant "husband," she assumed. She smiled at the man who was introduced as a trustee of the ranch and its manager for the past few years. He was around fifty, with a rather lived-in face, and his eyes were the most beautiful blue she'd ever seen.

She exchanged greetings with him.

"Leanne is our newest granddaughter-in-law," Garrett explained to Wayne, his voice filled with undisguised pleasure. "As soon as I get the rest of these boys married, then maybe we'll have a bunch of grandkids running around here." He gave Gina and Trent an approving glance.

Gina went pink, Leanne noted, experiencing a similar telltale heat in her cheeks. She'd never been worth a darn at maintaining a lie. Thinking of children, or rather, the making of them, had her squirming in her chair as if on the proverbial hot seat. She realized the depth of the deception on Cade's family and new waves of guilt overcame her.

Footsteps in the hall and the arrival of Cade delayed further discussion. He took the seat beside her, muttered hello to everyone in general and no one in particular.

Everyone helped themselves to platters of fajitas with beans and rice and, Leanne's favorite, guacamole dip. The conversation stayed on ranch business.

She gradually relaxed and ate the delicious meal, aware of the man at her side with every bite. She was astounded anew each time she thought of his shocking statement that morning. Electrical thrills ran over her body even now. She didn't know what Cade had told his grandfather and other Kincaid relatives, but they seemed to have taken the marriage in stride.

Scraping the last smidgen of guacamole onto her roll, she prepared to take the last bite. Without a break in his demeanor, Cade spooned the remaining dip from his plate onto hers in a gesture of husbandly sharing.

He met her startled gaze calmly.

For a minute she envisioned what marriage to him might be like. As a husband, he would be gentle, considerate…passionate…tender. She'd seen all those qualities in the time she'd been there.

Her heart went through its hitch-and-tap dance routine. Along with the excitement came an overweening sadness. She wished she could find a love of the kind she sensed Cade would give to his wife, and wondered if he had loved his fiancée very much.

That thought made her hurt someplace deep inside where dreams lived, but whether the pain was for him or herself, she didn't know.

"Are you through on the computer?" he asked, startling her out of the morose musing.

"I can quit if you need it."

"Actually I need you to help with the horses."

"Oh." She brightened. "Of course."

Garrett laughed and patted her hand. "Never saw a gal so thrilled at the chance of hard work. I believe you've got a keeper here, Cade."

Her heart stumbled to a stop.

Cade reached over and casually ruffled her hair. "Yep. I think you're right."

Again she felt the direct beam of several pairs of eyes. She couldn't quite look at anyone.

"And she blushes," Garrett said softly. "I never could resist a blushing woman."

"Me, either," Cade agreed, his tone going deeper.

She found her voice. "We'd better get to work."

The Kincaids laughed outright as she and Cade departed for the stables.

"Slow down," he drawled halfway across the quadrangle. "Here comes your kinfolk."

Rand and Suzanne, who held baby Joey, plus Mack and Bill, came toward them from the foreman's quarters.

Cade dropped an arm across her shoulders. "Courage, Braveheart," he murmured. "We're outnumbered, but we're the toughest of the bunch."

She had to smile. The smile became genuine when she spoke to Suzanne and Suzanne's seventeen-year-old brother, Mack. She turned to her youngest nephew and held out her hands.

"Will you come to Auntie Leanne?" she crooned. She gave him a big grin and clucked her tongue at him.

He held out his arms and came readily to her, giving her his four-toothed smile.

"Any more teeth yet?" she asked.

Suzanne shook her head. "I've decided he's going

to be a chipmunk all his life. And have to be carried around all the time, too. He refuses to walk.''

''He's not ready. Are you, big fella?'' She teased the baby. ''Don't let them push you into anything—''

She stopped abruptly, but couldn't take the words back. Rand and Bill stiffened. Suzanne and Mack looked uncomfortable. She'd accused the two men of doing that to her on the aborted wedding day. Guilt ate at her for the hateful things she'd said. She didn't know why she'd been so frightened and defiant.

Perhaps if she'd sat down and spoken about her concerns quietly they could have resolved the problems then. Maybe Bill would have understood and agreed to wait. Instead, she'd felt pushed to the wall.

But that was no excuse for what she'd done—leaving at the last minute, going back on her word, causing trouble for everyone. She glanced at the tall, silent male who had come to her rescue.

Now he was involved, too, and they had to live a lie. All because of her. She wanted to apologize and tell her family how very much she cared for them— all of them, including their oldest and dearest friend. She wanted to erase the hurt and embarrassment she'd caused.

But there was no going back. As her brother had so grimly stated, she'd made her bed.

Joey patted her cheek and gave her a drooly grin. Her heart overflowed with simple, uncomplicated love for him. If only all relationships could be this easy. She pressed her face into his sweet-smelling neck and kissed him until he giggled in delight.

''We're going to check the horses for sell,'' Cade

said to Rand. "You want to review them for any you think we ought to keep to stock the new remuda?"

Leanne couldn't help but admire Cade. That was a nice thing for him to do. Her brother had been foreman at the Kincaid ranch for a few years, and she was certain he had to be wondering about his position what with all the newfound Kincaid heirs coming onto the scene. Cade had acknowledged Rand's position in a gracious but businesslike manner.

The security of her brother's job was another worry to add to all the others.

"That's it," Cade announced at six. "You can go on to the house. The main house," he added.

Leanne sighed in relief. They had examined every horse in the sale bunch and treated each and every one of them for worms, one for a small cut and others for various minor ailments. Cade wanted them in top shape for the auction, which was two weeks away. It had been a hard day…in more ways than one.

Thanks to a fractious mare who had stepped on her foot, she limped toward the house, fatigue trailing at her heels. She was too tired to worry about sharing a room with her pretend husband. All she wanted was a hot shower, food, then sleep.

In that order.

She entered Cade's room by the verandah's side door. The long Spanish-style verandah, which ran the length of the house, was the perfect place for a husband and wife to sit and relax while watching the twilight overtake the day.

Husband? She doubted she would ever share a life with anyone.

Feeling decidedly sorry for herself and trying not to, she headed straight for the bath. She dropped her clothes to the floor before turning the shower on full and hot.

"Ah-hh," she breathed, letting it cascade over her hair and down her back.

She washed leisurely, then rinsed and dried off. Wrapping a towel around her head, she opened the door to the bedroom and went to her canvas bag. There she hesitated, wondering if she had to dress for dinner or if she could sneak down to the kitchen and bring something back to the room. The latter sounded more appealing.

After pulling out a new sweat suit in a luscious mossy green, she slipped it on. No need for underclothes. She'd sleep in the sweats tonight instead of the long T-shirt she usually wore. That way Cade wouldn't get any ideas—

"You finished in the shower?" a male voice asked.

She nearly jumped out of her skin. Spinning around, she spotted him in the easy chair, his boots off and lined up next to the wall, and demanded, "What are you doing here?"

"I happen to sleep here."

He made a leisurely perusal down, then up, her body. When he met her gaze, she gasped at the heat in his eyes. She felt consumed. Worse, she wanted to be.

"I—I didn't expect you in this soon," she stammered.

"Obviously." His smile was thin, mocking. "I hadn't fully appreciated the delights available to a husband until this moment."

"You could have alerted me to your presence."
She thought of him watching her, his gaze like living
coals on her flesh as she stood there, naked, deciding
what to wear. She melted inside, her body going soft
and damp and ready.

"Why?"

She refused to be daunted by the hunger in his
eyes. "So I could have held my tummy in. All women
do that when they know men are watching them."

He laughed out loud, then stood and closed the distance between them. He touched her cheek, his fingertips cool on her skin. She was startled at how hot
she was, at how much she wanted him. Her gaze
flicked to the bed.

When she looked back at him, the laughter had
disappeared. Now there was only dark, liquid fire
shadowing his eyes, burning her with its intensity.

"We can go there," he said quietly.

"W-where?"

Cade glanced at the bed, then back to her.
"There."

She shook her head, nearly dislodging the towel
that covered her wet hair. "No."

"Coward." He was shocked to realize how much
he wanted her to agree, how much he wanted her,
period. Sex had never been the driving force in his
life. There had been other dreams more important
than physical demands.

Right now, he couldn't recall a one of them.

The vision of her slender body and its perfect form,
the willowy grace as she moved, filled his mind. She
bit down on her bottom lip the way she did when she

was troubled. It set off new explosions of need inside him.

"I want your mouth," he whispered, leaning closer. "I want it under mine, moving with mine."

"No."

"That isn't the word I want to hear," he said, his voice softer, sexier. Needier. He cupped a hand around her neck. "I want to hear you saying yes...yes...*yes*."

Leanne tried to look away. He mesmerized her with his eyes, bringing her completely under his sensual spell.

"It would be good, I promise you that."

She could almost believe him, in spite of her contrary previous experience. She licked her dry, burning lips. "You shouldn't tempt me," she said, and wished he would.

He released her abruptly. "Aren't women ever capable of making up their minds and keeping them that way?"

Without waiting for an answer, he went into the bathroom and closed the door none too gently.

Letting out a shaky breath, she collapsed onto the end of the bed. The way he made her feel, all achy and burning, worried her. Oh, how she'd wanted to say *yes* and to heck with the consequences.

After brushing out her wet hair, she put a band around it and went to the kitchen. There she asked if she could prepare a plate and take it to her room. The housekeeper shooed her out with the promise to send a meal to her room.

Ten minutes later the woman and her son arrived with two trays. They arranged plates of food, along with salads and a basket of rolls, on a lamp table next to the wall, then left a tray propped behind the table.

"Set the dishes on the tray and put it in the hall when you're finished," she told Leanne with a sweet smile.

Blushing furiously, Leanne thanked them and gulped as she viewed the candle, already lit, and the single rose in a crystal vase. The housekeeper must have thought she was serving a honeymoon dinner. As soon as they left, she tossed the rose in the trash can and bent to blow out the candle.

"Leave it," Cade suggested, coming out of the bathroom.

He wore new-looking pajama bottoms. She knew at once it wasn't his usual night attire. She groaned silently as her imagination fed sensuous images into her mind.

Barefoot, he crossed the room and looked over the two plates. "Steak tartare, roasted potatoes, asparagus. Looks good." He pulled a chair closer to the table, then bent toward the wastebasket. "What's this?"

"A rose," she said grimly.

He glanced from her to the flower to the vase. He replaced the rose. "There. Romantic, huh?"

"I'm not in any mood for your sarcastic humor."

His eyes darkened. "Maybe I'm not in the mood for your sour disposition. Ol' Bill was lucky you ran out on him."

"I didn't run! I told him I was leaving and that I wouldn't be at the church. Oh, never mind." It didn't matter what she said, Cade, as well as Rand and Bill, would put his own twist to it.

When Cade held the chair and indicated she should be seated, she did.

They ate the excellent meal in total silence. Cade set the dishes on the tray and put it outside the door. When he closed it, he turned back to the room and surveyed her.

"I'm going to catch the news," he said.

He proceeded to turn on a TV in a wall unit, then flopped one pillow on another against the headboard and settled on the bed to watch.

She stayed glued to the chair throughout the news and a movie. They watched young Hornblower fight pirates and fall in love with a woman he could never have while aboard ship. When the movie was over, Cade brushed his teeth and lay down on the bed.

"Where am I going to sleep?" she finally asked.

He glanced at the other side of the queen-size bed. "There's plenty of room."

"I'm not going to sleep with you."

"Why not?"

"Because we're not married and if we share a bed, it might lead to...complications." She plumped up her shaky resolve. "I am not going to become involved with you."

He eyed her for a long minute that sent her blood to boiling. "Married seems pretty involved to me."

She jumped to her feet and paced the floor. "We're not married! I wish you'd stop saying that!"

"Then you'd better tell your brother and boyfriend, or else they're going to think the worst come morning."

"They already think the worst. Thanks to you," she reminded him, angered anew. She threw her hands into the air in frustration. "How do I keep getting into these situations?" she demanded.

"You've done this before?" He sounded only mildly interested.

"Of course not!" She sank back into the chair in defeat. "It's men. You're so damn difficult to deal with. Females can clone females. We don't really need men at all. The world would be a better place. Peaceful."

"Dull," he corrected.

His eyes moved over her, stabbing her with the hot desire she could see in them. She felt the softening inside. The conflict and the anger came down to this, she realized. To the hunger between them.

As she watched, his body hardened, his erection visible beneath the thin cotton pajamas. Fires burned out of control within her. Breathing became difficult.

She hated him for doing this to her. She hated the need she couldn't seem to control anymore. She hated—

Closing her eyes, she admitted the truth. She didn't hate him at all. She wanted to crawl into that bed with him. She wanted the bliss he promised, the door into passion that he'd opened for her, showing her a glimpse of paradise. It wasn't him she didn't trust. It was herself.

"If you won't leave, then I will," she said, deciding retreat was the better part of valor.

"The hell you will," he snarled in a low, deep voice with no anger in it, only conviction.

She clenched her hands into fists. "I have to. This isn't right. I can't have sex with you and pretend a lie. I can't, Cade. I—"

"All right," he said. "I get the picture."

He flung himself off the bed and, grabbing some clothing, went into the bathroom. She put on socks and sneakers, but needed her things from the bathroom before she could return to the bunkhouse.

When Cade emerged, he was dressed. He took one look at her shoes. "I'm leaving. You can stay."

Shocked, she asked, "Where are you going?"

"What the hell does it matter?" He yanked on his boots, grabbed a jacket, and was gone.

She went out onto the verandah and watched him stride across to the stable. In a few minutes he left, riding the stallion that was his pride and joy. She didn't know whether she felt relief or anger.

Retreating to the room—carefully leaving the door unlocked in case he returned—she turned out the lamp and climbed into the bed. It seemed big and empty. Lonely.

Tears stung her eyes and nose. She couldn't for the life of her figure out why she was so upset. Cade was acting the perfect gentleman—which was exactly what she'd asked of him.

Chills and heat danced over her skin in alternate waves as visions of him raced through her mind. Her body tensed as she recalled the pleasure of his kisses and caresses. Since the first moment she'd met him, something had changed within her.

As if a door were opening for the first time, she began to understand the restless, irresistible pull of nature between a man and woman. Understand? She longed for it. And that wouldn't do, not at all. Cade must think she was a very unreliable person. She thought so herself.

She sighed shakily and wished for wisdom to handle the coming days. She didn't want to hurt anyone, either Bill or her family and, most of all, Cade, her rough but gallant knight.

Sleep was a long time coming.

Eight

Cade entered the bedroom shortly before the sun rose. He paused at the door and removed his boots. Crossing the room in his socks, he stopped by the bed, unable to keep from observing his sleeping "wife."

Every nerve in his body clenched at the thought.

She lay curled on her side in the place he usually slept. Her face was snuggled into his pillow.

There was something about a sleeping woman. This one looked particularly young and vulnerable, as well as soft and desirable. She brought out oddly protective emotions in him that made no sense. And stirred his libido into a hot lava pool of seething hunger.

He didn't like that, but neither did he like the subtle coercion her brother and ex-fiancé exerted. They used her love for them to sway her to their way of thinking. He could imagine the pressure on her to agree to the marriage.

Kneeling beside the bed, he touched the tangle of thick dark hair because he suddenly needed to.

Braveheart. She was that, in her own way, even if she didn't know it. She was careful with those she loved. It was a facet he'd never considered in a relationship.

It caught his attention.

She sighed in her sleep and turned her head. He let go of her hair until she settled, then he ran his fingers into the waves, combing them into order.

Her eyes opened.

He was caught in the bewitching freshness of a mossy green stare. He smiled.

She did, too. For an instant. Before she remembered the distress that had brought her to this point…and his bed. He saw worry leap into the verdant depths of her gaze, dimming the springtime brightness.

She sat up and scooted away from him until her back was against the headboard. "You're home."

He nodded.

She glanced at the bed, empty except for her. "Where did you sleep?"

"At the line shack."

"I'm sorry—"

He stopped her with a kiss, a brush of his lips over hers. She turned her head, clearly embarrassed. She wasn't used to waking with a man. He liked that.

"It's past dawn. Time to get busy. I'll bring some coffee in."

"Bring breakfast," she requested. "That way I won't have to face your grandfather with our lies."

He left to fetch plates of scrambled eggs and bacon, toast, orange juice and coffee. The housekeeper smiled broadly when he insisted on carrying the tray to the room himself.

As he'd expected, Leanne was up and dressed, as nervous as a displaced mountain lion. "Relax. I'm not going to bite. Yet." But he was feeling more and more in the mood.

"I'll bite back."

Mouthy female. She wasn't going to give an inch.

"I'll look forward to it," he drawled, deliberately teasing her, liking the way her eyes flared with interest she couldn't hide. "When we make love," he added under his breath.

"We won't."

She had moved silently across the carpet and, he now realized, was standing behind him as he unloaded the tray. "You weren't supposed to hear that," he told her on a note of wry laughter.

"Cade—"

He rounded on her. He didn't want to hear her reasons on why they weren't going to make love. Tossing the tray to the bed, he pulled her against him. He just had time to see the startled look in her eyes before he closed his and kissed the daylights out of her.

To his surprise, she didn't fight. Instead she kissed him back, sending his conscience into a state of stunned shock and his libido into a state of raging hunger. He tugged her hips to his and went weak-kneed with pleasure.

He groaned and released her mouth. "Lady, what you do to me. Drives me right to the wall."

She nodded, then pressed her forehead to his chest. He could feel the uncertainty that trembled in her slender body along with the passion they'd created.

"We're going to drink fully of this cup," he promised.

"But should we?" she questioned. "We're not married or committed to each other in any way."

"It's something I don't think we should miss. We'd

regret it the rest of our lives, and then we would always wonder if something good had slipped by us.''

She sighed, stepped back and took a chair at the table. ''We'd better eat, then get busy. I understand the remuda boss is a real demon for work.''

''He might make an exception in your case.''

''I don't want him to,'' she said, the simplicity of the statement stopping any arguments he might have made.

The worry was back in her eyes. It bothered him, although he couldn't say why. He sensed a sadness in her that was at odds with her spunky way of facing life.

Intrigued, he wondered what made her tick...and why he wanted to find out.

Leanne listened intently while Cade explained what he wanted done.

''We're going to work each horse until it's tired, at least an hour. I want them divided into seasoned and green, sweet and ornery. Next week we'll work with the green ones. By auction day, I don't want any surprises about any horse's temper or ability to perform. Got it?''

''Right.''

He flicked her a sharp glance. ''That's ninety-eight horses. We'll be working sixty hours each of the next two weeks.''

''Or more.''

''Or more,'' he agreed. ''You don't seem displeased.''

She grinned. ''I'll love it.''

''Huh. This won't be a picnic.''

He mounted one of the geldings and let himself out the gate into the paddock where a small bunch of cows and calves milled about, uneasy at being removed from the herd.

Leanne climbed on the gelding she was to test. First she opened and closed the gate from horseback, which depended on the animal knowing what the rider wanted and doing his part by standing close to the gate, walking through as it swung open, then moving into position so the rider could refasten it. Then she put the cutting horse through the rest of its paces—backing it, asking it to spin in place and checking its response to rein and knee pressure as well as body position. She pretended to fall and hung off the side. The horse stopped and stood quietly until she was firmly back in the saddle.

She and Cade each cut a cow-calf pair from the rest and had their mounts hold them for a full minute before letting them return to the herd. They lassoed and tied yearlings while the horses kept the rope taut. After an hour, they left the animals ground-hitched while they saddled up the next pair, then they consulted.

"Seasoned," she told him of the gelding she'd ridden. "Sweet."

"Same here."

He moved the two mounts to one of the arena pastures, then swung up on the next one. They repeated the whole procedure. They spent five hours in the saddle, then headed toward the bunkhouse for lunch. Rand met her on the way.

"Suzanne set a place for you at our house," he

said. He cast a glare in Cade's direction. "He's invited, too."

"Good," Cade said. "I go where my wife goes."

She felt his heat at her back and knew he'd stepped close as soon as her brother appeared. "We'll be right there," she promised. "We'll, uh, wash up first."

Rand hesitated, then walked off.

Cade took her arm and headed for the main house. "Say whatever's on your mind."

"Don't quarrel with my brother," she requested, giving him a beseeching glance. "Or Bill. No matter what they say."

"That's a tall order."

"They're probably going to ask you some questions. Rand may want to know how you plan to support me or something equally obnoxious. Bill might tell you to treat me right or else. They've been looking after me all my life."

"Yeah, men tend to take care of their own."

His tone was so repressive she didn't continue the discussion, but she found herself avidly curious about him. She wondered about the people he loved, those he considered his "own." She wondered how it would feel to be loved by this man.

"Cade, did you love the woman who left you at the altar very much?" she asked as they stepped on the verandah.

He gave her an oblique glance. "What brought that on?"

She stopped and gazed at the hills as she thought. "I don't know. It's just…sometimes I'm not sure I know what love means. I don't understand relationships. The male-female thing."

"Who does?" He held the door open for her to precede him into his room. When he tossed his hat onto a bed post, so did she. They went into the bathroom. Cade took one sink and she took the other.

"Is it merely a physical attraction that we glorify by calling it love and making it a grand thing, eulogized in song and poem and story? Or is it the sweet yearning of the soul for its mate?" She stared at him through their reflected images in the mirror. "What do you think?"

He gave his usual sardonic smile. "I think we're wasting time. Your brother is expecting us. If we don't arrive soon, he and his sidekick will probably come looking. We wouldn't want either of them to think we're indulging in matrimonial pleasures, would we?"

Turning on the water, he splashed his face, then lathered it. Fascinated, she watched as an intense yearning grew inside her. She wanted his kisses, his gentle but exciting touch, his soft murmuring in her ear. She wanted the full taste of pleasure she instinctively knew would be hers if they made love. She wanted *him.*

A hot blush speared through her whole body. "Love can't be simply an attraction between the sexes, can it?"

He rinsed his face, then looked at her in the mirror, his eyes questioning. "What is it you want to know?"

Water beaded on his tanned skin. It ran down the twin lines beside his mouth and dripped off his chin. She suppressed an urge to snuggle into his arms and catch the drops with her tongue. She wanted desperately to kiss him.

"I don't know," she murmured, looking down as tears burned behind her eyes. She bent and wet her face. When she reached out, he put the soap in her hand.

They washed up quickly, sharing the single bar of soap without words. He tossed her a towel, then dried his face and hands on a matching one.

"I think love is composed of many parts," he told her, neatly hanging up the towel. "First comes the sexual attraction. That's what brings people together so they can get to know each other. They learn to trust each other by sharing things—"

"What things?"

He flicked her a sideways glance that left her steaming with desire, then he grinned. "Laughter. Their deepest thoughts. Their worries. Their hopes and dreams. If there's a significant level of mutual interest, then they commit to each other."

"By having sex?"

"Making love is one way. By standing up in front of their friends and family and making it known that they plan to build a life together is another."

"Marriage."

"Yes, marriage."

"Bill and I shared all those things, but I still didn't want to marry him. Do you think something is wrong with me? Maybe I'm incapable of committing to the long term, the way a lot of men are supposed to be."

"Men commit when it's the right woman, the right time and the right circumstances. When those three come together, so will you."

Her heart bucked and plunged as he explained his idea of love and marriage. She wanted all that he described. However, she didn't think those things would ever come together for her. She pushed the thought aside and tried for a lighter note as they left his quarters. "Thanks, doc. How much do you charge for advice?"

"*Nada.* For you, it's free."

He was back to his sardonic mode. She liked his wry sense of humor, she realized. It went with his Gilas drawl and laid-back manner.

As they crossed the road and walked the short distance to the foreman's house, Cade spoke again, this time in answer to her earlier worry. "I promise I won't sock either of them, no matter what questions they ask or remarks they make."

"Thank you." She sighed in relief at his vow. "I'm not going to say anything hateful, either. No matter what Rand says."

"Famous last words," he murmured.

They glanced at each other as they climbed the two steps onto the porch leading into the kitchen and smiled in total understanding. Leanne knocked to be polite, then led the way inside.

Mack held his crying nephew while Suzanne, looking harried, dished up the noon meal. "Hi, come on in. Dinner in two shakes," she told them.

Leanne noticed that a roast held pride of place on the table and filled the room with a delicious aroma. She realized she was starved. "Here, let me help. What do you want me to do?"

Suzanne gave her a grateful smile. "Take the corn sticks out of the oven before they burn."

"Sure thing. Mack, why don't you and Joey take

Cade into the living room? I hear the TV. Rand and Bill must be catching the weather report.''

Cade followed Mack and the baby out of the kitchen. Leanne put on an oven mitt and rescued the corn sticks. After dumping them into the napkin-lined basket on the counter, she stirred the creamed corn, then tasted it, keeping an ear tuned to the living room in case trouble erupted.

Not that she expected any, but it didn't hurt to be alert, as her father used to say.

"This is done," she told Suzanne, getting a bowl from the cabinet. "This one okay?"

"Yes." Suzanne tore salad greens into bite-size pieces. She gave Leanne a thoughtful appraisal.

"Have I got egg on my face or something?"

Suzanne's mouth tilted up at the corners. "Rand is having a hard time thinking of his little sister as a married woman." She laughed softly. "I think this is going to be a good experience for him."

"How so?"

"Everyone has to learn to let go of the ones they love. I'd like him to get the lesson down pat before Joey gets to the rebellious stage and strikes out on his own." She poured dressing on the salad and began tossing it.

Leanne set the big oak table. They worked comfortably with each other as they put the food out.

"It's nice having another female here," Suzanne commented as they finished. "There're so few of us. Until Gina came, it was only me. People think the ranch is cursed. Families don't want to stay. Do you think you and Cade will live here?"

Leanne didn't quite know what to say. Dismissing

a lie, she spoke from the heart. "I would love it, but I don't know exactly what our plans are."

Suzanne surveyed the table. "I think that's it. Dinner," she called through to the living room.

Leanne waited nervously for the men to enter. She heard the TV go off, then the collective footsteps as the four men trooped into the kitchen. Rand carried his son.

After strapping Joey into a high chair, Rand gestured for Cade to take a seat on one side of the table and Bill to sit on the other. Mack took the chair next to Bill. That left the one beside Cade open.

Instead of sitting as the other men did, Cade waited until Leanne set the bread basket on the table, then held the chair for her. Prickles skimmed up and down her neck as she accepted the place next to her pretend husband. His light touch on her nape was reassuring.

Glancing up, she met Bill's hard gaze. He, too, had seen the subtle caress. She felt his anger and sensed his frustration. An apology stuck on the tip of her tongue. She didn't know what to say to him.

"I noticed the clouds gathering over the mountains," Suzanne said into the uneasy silence after they were all seated. "Are we in for another storm today?"

"Tonight, most likely, and tomorrow," Rand said.

The talk stayed generally on the weather and ranching problems. Near the end of the meal, Rand cleared his throat and looked directly at Cade. "You planning on living here at the ranch?"

"Assuming Garrett is able to buy the place, yes."

"Wayne and Sterling have filled me in on that," Rand said, nodding.

Leanne had met Wayne but before she could ask

about the other man, Bill spoke up. "Who are they?" he asked, interest springing into his eyes.

"Wayne Kincaid is one of the trustees for Jennifer McCallum, along with Jenny's adoptive father, Sterling McCallum," Rand explained. He went on to outline the complicated connections to the Kincaid ranch. "Jenny is six, the youngest—as far as anyone knows—of old Jeremiah Kincaid's illegitimate kids."

He paused as if realizing that Cade was also a Kincaid bastard—Larry's. Leanne tensed. If Rand or Bill made any remarks about Cade and his birth, she wasn't sure Cade could uphold his promise. Luckily her brother stuck to ranch history.

"She inherited the ranch after Lexine Baxter killed off her father-in-law and her husband. Dugin Kincaid was the only known legitimate heir at that time. Wayne was thought to be dead, killed in Vietnam. He came back to Whitehorn a few years ago."

Suzanne smiled at her husband. "Thank goodness that terrible Lexine didn't decide you might know too much and have to be disposed of, too."

Rand met his wife's gaze. His face softened into a smile that first appeared in his eyes. Leanne felt their love as a tangible thing.

Cade was right. It was more than sex. But how did a person know for sure it was love?

She covertly studied Bill, then Cade. When she thought of her longtime friend, she definitely felt warmth. He had helped her through some rough patches in her life.

Affection? Yes, definitely. Love? Sort of. But not the kind that led to marriage.

The certainty stole over her. She had been right to

tell him they shouldn't marry. It would never have worked. She didn't love him the way Rand and Suzanne loved each other. She didn't yearn for him or miss him when he wasn't around. She didn't think of him very often.

Her eyes were drawn irresistibly to Cade. His dark eyes, sprinkled with green and lined with gold, gazed back at her. Neither spoke, but the tension was there, the pull of man to woman, woman to man.

Their voices dwindled into the background as the conversation centered on the Baxter woman dressing in an assortment of Indian ceremonial clothes and scaring the stuffing out of old Homer Gilmore, a prospector who had thought aliens had landed, and any others who ventured into the woods where she was searching for some fabled sapphire mine.

"Dessert," Suzanne said.

Leanne was plummeted back to reality as her sister-in-law placed slices of homemade chocolate pie in front of her and Cade. "This looks delicious."

"She's the best cook this side of the Mississippi," Rand declared.

Leanne smiled at the pride he took in his wife. Her big brother surprised her in many ways as a married man. He was more thoughtful and considerate than he used to be. Maybe there was something to the myth about love taming the savage beast.

She looked at Cade and wondered if she wanted him tamed. Wild was so exciting...

Ever aware of his pretend wife, Cade glanced at her in time see a grin flit over her face before she suppressed a laugh.

What amused her about murder and Indian curses

and all the rest of the baggage that went with the Kincaid name?

His host brought the conversation back to the topic evidently very much on his mind. "What if the sale doesn't go through and Garrett Kincaid changes his mind about buying the ranch for all his grandsons? What will you do about Leanne in that case?"

The question brought his hackles up. "I'd expect my wife to go wherever I do. I'd expect her to work along with me so that maybe we could buy a spread of our own one day."

Rand and his friend Bill looked patently displeased with his reply. Cade mentally shrugged. They didn't particularly please him, either.

"No wonder you and Leanne fell immediately in love," Suzanne put in, delight in her smile. "You both have the same dreams. That's wonderful."

Cade relaxed at the open approval from Leanne's sister-in-law. At least there was one person at the table who might be on his side. He cast a sideways glance at Leanne. He wasn't sure where his "wife" stood on the subject.

She'd appeared startled by Suzanne's words. Now she looked somewhat introspective but pleased. He couldn't decide what this meant. If anything.

Bah. Who knew what women were thinking? They were as unpredictable as the wind off the Crazy Mountains.

They finished dessert with only some minor skirmishes. Cade answered all of Rand's questions evasively, but remained pleasant in spite of the ex-fiancé's scowl, which grew fiercer as the conversation wore on. At last he and Leanne could leave with the excuse of work to be done before the storm moved in.

"You handled that very well," Leanne complimented him, giving his arm a squeeze as they headed for the paddock.

It was an odd sort of pleasure, almost an ache, that settled inside Cade. He didn't know exactly what that feeling meant, but he knew it was worrisome.

Leanne coaxed the mare through the door of the arena. "Good girl," she crooned, rubbing the animal's neck.

With the storm fast approaching, Cade had decided to move into the building and keep working. That suited her. Dealing with the horses left her little time for thinking about Cade and the situation they were in.

She had the horse back up, pivot, spring forward, cut a cow from a group and hold it. The mare did the work, but not willingly. She grabbed at the bit and frequently shook her head. Leanne marked her down as "seasoned but temperamental" and released her in the designated paddock. Before she could exit the gate, the mare reached out and bit her on the shoulder.

Surprised, Leanne emitted a yelp of pain. She gave a hard downward yank on the mare's head to let her know this was not acceptable behavior, then exited.

"Leanne! Are you okay?" Bill rushed up to her.

She managed a faint smile. "Well, for someone just bitten by a cantankerous horse, I'm fine." She headed for the tack room in the stable.

"How bad is it?" he asked, trailing along with her. "We'd better check it out."

She lifted her shirt away from her shoulder and peered at the wound. Teeth marks curved in an interesting pattern of red over her skin, which wasn't broken. Bruises were starting to form. "It's nothing."

"Nothing," Bill scoffed. "You could have been seriously injured. Where's the liniment?"

"In that cabinet." She pointed with her chin while she gingerly checked the soreness of her shoulder muscles and felt her collarbone.

"Can you move your arm and shoulder? You could have a broken collarbone." Bill found a bottle of horse liniment in a cabinet.

"I think it's okay." She felt a little shaky. Her shoulder hurt worse than she wanted him to know.

"Take your shirt off. I'll rub this in."

Once she would have followed his orders without a thought to propriety or modesty, but now she found herself reluctant to expose even her shoulder. "I can take care of it," she told him.

"Don't be stupid. I want to check that bite out."

"No," she said firmly. "I'll handle it. I'm not a child."

He glared at her, impatience in every line of his body. "Then stop acting like one."

Still she hesitated. She wasn't really Cade's wife, so nothing had really changed, but she felt funny about other men, including a childhood friend, touching her now that she was supposed to be a married woman.

On the other hand, being married, even if it had been real, didn't mean Cade had put his brand on her. Bill was simply trying to help her, as he'd always done. She probably was being silly.

But when Bill reached for the top button of her shirt, she shied away. "Don't," she said, a warning in the word that surprised her. She hadn't realized she would feel this strongly about being touched without permission.

He snorted but paid no attention.

"I believe my wife told you to back off," a male voice declared in a deceptively lazy drawl.

Cade opened the door the rest of the way and entered. He looked dangerous. In the dim light shadows formed sharp angles under his high cheekbones.

When she met his eyes, Leanne realized he was dangerous. Anger glinted from his eyes, directed at the man next to her.

Cade closed the space between them and put himself between her and Bill. "When a lady says no, it means no. Don't ever ignore my wife's wishes again. You understand?"

Bill's mouth thinned. "I was concerned about her. Leanne and I have been...friends..." He paused to put an insinuating twist to the word. "...all our lives. In our part of the country, friends look after each other."

"She has a husband now. I'll look after her. Touch her again and you'll be picking yourself up out of a manure pile, *friend*."

Bill's hands clenched. Cade shifted into a fighting stance, his legs spread and braced, ready for an attack. Leanne stepped between them.

"I think I need to lie down," she murmured to Cade, acting the fragile female to ward off further trouble.

He flicked her a glance, his face softening. "All

right. I want to check that shoulder. Ice will stop the swelling. Liniment shouldn't be used for forty-eight hours on a bruise,'' he added with another warning glance at Bill.

Leanne leaned against him so that he had to take part of her weight. He put an arm around her shoulders and led her outside and across the quadrangle to the main house. He took her to their room and sat her on the bed before unfastening her shirt.

"Damn," Cade said upon lifting her collar and examining her shoulder. "That was a wicked bite. I'll shoot the horse that did it," he promised, only half joking.

He realized he didn't like her being injured any more than he liked her being bullied.

"I'll get that ice pack." He headed for the kitchen and was back in thirty seconds with a bag of frozen peas.

She laughed and let him remove the shirt and place the bag on the bruises rapidly forming on her smooth-as-cream skin. She laid her head against his stomach. "Thanks for rescuing me. Again."

He felt her breath through his shirt, then he felt her mouth. She pressed several kisses along his waist, right above his belly button. His breath froze.

"I didn't know that was an erogenous zone," he murmured. "Any place you touch probably is."

When she slipped one arm around him, he didn't protest the embrace. "Leanne?" he said, not sure what he was asking.

"Make love to me, Cade," she whispered. "I need you to make love to me."

The words hung in the air between them. The house was silent as if it waited to see what he would do. He wondered about that himself.

Nine

"**Y**ou'd better give that a second thought, maybe a third," Cade suggested softly.

Leanne shook her head. "It's all I've been thinking about for days. Did you...do you have protection?"

She couldn't believe she'd asked that. But then, she could discuss anything with Cade. He might be cynical at times, but he took her seriously.

His glance went to the bedside table, and she knew the answer to her question. She hugged him hard and pressed her face against him.

"I want you so," she whispered. "It's like an ache inside that never leaves. Make it go away, Cade. Make love to me."

Against her cheek, she felt his chest rise, then heard him expel the deep breath. His hands touched her hair. When he buried his fingers in the unruly strands, she relaxed and closed her eyes.

"Let's get the rest of these out of the way," he murmured, moving to her clothing.

"Yes."

He helped her first, then she helped him. Other than her nephew, she'd never undressed a male. She wanted to explore and stroke and kiss each part of Cade as it was revealed. When she proceeded to do just that, he caught her chin and tipped her face up to gaze into her eyes.

"Keep that up and I won't last a minute," he warned.

But his eyes were laughing. She laughed, too. "This is going to be wonderful."

"As wonderful as I can make it," he promised in a husky, thrilling tone. "This one's for you."

With that, he lifted her in his arms and, after sweeping the bedspread and sheet aside, laid her in the bed. She lifted her arms to him when he paused to let his gaze wander over her. Heat rushed to her skin, following each point where his eyes lingered.

"You make me hot when you look at me like that."

"It makes me hot, too."

She could see that. His body was erect, ready for completion. Sensations pulsed through her in heated waves. "Come to me," she invited.

He smiled and slid down to lay beside her on his side, one hand going behind her neck. His mouth claimed hers in a rampaging kiss that spoke of hunger and needs long left unattended...and other things she couldn't read.

"You have the most beautiful body," he whispered, his free hand roaming over her in gentle forays that set little suns to flaming everywhere he touched.

He settled on her rib cage below her breasts. With his thumbs, he stroked the undersides of her breasts. She lifted toward him, wanting more.

"I can't think," she told him, pressing kisses along his neck as he nibbled on her earlobe.

"You don't have to. Just relax and let me have my way with you."

His soft laughter tickled her ear. Laughing with him, feeling deliriously happy, she lifted her face and sought his mouth. He let her take the kiss, then turned it into one of mutual feasting.

She welcomed his tongue and stroked it with hers. She bit at his lips. He licked hers. Spirals of electricity whirled into the infinite spaces inside her, dazzling her with bright flashes of color.

Magic. His hands were magic.

He stroked her breasts, circled the nipples, gathered one into his palm, kneaded until she tingled and ached for more from him. His mouth followed his hands, sucking at her breasts until they tingled in pleasure that soaked right down to the most intimate part of her.

Time lost all meaning. The universe narrowed until it enclosed only the two of them. Reality was each other. Everything else disappeared.

"I've never felt like this," she whispered, running her fingers into his thick, gleaming hair that smelled of shampoo and sunshine.

"You'll feel even better," he promised, lifting his head to observe the effects of his handiwork. "You have the most perfect breasts I've ever seen. I've wanted to do this since that night at the cabin."

He bent, took a nipple into his mouth, and brushed his tongue over it while sucking at the same time.

She clutched his shoulders and held on. "My dress slipped. I was embarrassed. Did you think me wanton?"

"No." He gazed into her eyes. "I thought you

were frightened—not of me but of something you'd left behind."

"My family. And my fiancé," she added. "I was afraid they would talk me into going through with the wedding." She caught her bottom lip between her teeth as she realized that was the truth. "You must think me a spineless creature."

"You did what you had to. As to what I think..."

His eyes moved over her in a hungry foray. The hot stare stole her breath away. She put a hand over his eyes.

"Don't. I can't breathe when you look at me that way," she protested.

He kissed the center of her palm, then pushed her hand to the mattress and held it there. He kissed her mouth and each breast, then down her body to her navel. He played there for a minute and moved on.

"Cade?" she said when he pressed his face into the curly mound at the junction of her thighs.

"This is going to be good," he said, glancing up at her. "I promise you'll like it. So will I."

Her eyes widened when he bent to her, his mouth finding her most intimate place. She gasped when he flicked his tongue over the sensitive nub. When he sucked, she emitted a tiny cry of surprise.

"This is...I've never felt this. Oh, Cade, it's the most intense sensation..."

He slipped his hands under her hips, lifting her to him, stroking her constantly so that the pleasure never faded, but grew and grew until she was gasping.

She tensed when he moved again, stroking inside her and outside at the same time, filling her with more sensation than she could bear. She gasped his name.

"Easy, love. It's only going to get better. Tell me anything you don't like."

"Everything is wonderful, so much feeling...and the tension...I've never felt this way. I want you. Come to me now." The miracle of it rushed through her, this wonderful passion, the sharing of it, this wanting to take and to give at the same time.

"Not yet. I want you to have more. I want to give you pleasure you'll never forget."

His voice was raw, rough with male desire. He bent to her again. His mouth and his finger moved in unison. She squeezed her eyes tightly closed and clutched the sheet as her blood ran hot and rampant, wildly out of her control and totally in his.

And she didn't care. Later she would need to think about that, but not now. At this moment she was beyond thought. She could only react to his delicious caresses inside and outside her body.

She writhed and twisted and cried out as wave after wave of need flashed through her. "Cade, I want...I want..."

He moved more vigorously, surfeiting her with sensation upon sensation. She stopped breathing.

The waves mounted, higher and higher yet.

"Trust me," he murmured against her hot flesh. "Let yourself go. Take all you need from me."

"Don't stop," she pleaded. "I'm—"

There were no words for what happened next. With another caress from him, a sun seemed to explode inside her, causing her to cry out in surprised delight.

Cade felt the coiled release and nearly came unglued himself. She was the most natural lover he'd ever had, giving herself to him and the pleasure in total trust.

He moved up beside her when the tension was gone completely and let her rest. "You've never had that before," he murmured, unable to keep the pride out of his voice.

"Never," she vowed. She pressed wild kisses all over his chest. "It was the most wonderful thing imaginable. You have no idea—"

He grinned when she stopped abruptly. A beguiling blush bloomed in her cheeks.

"I think I have an inkling," he assured her.

When he laughed, she tilted her head back and gazed at him with an expression in her eyes that drove a hot poker of need straight down inside him.

"I want to be in you now," he said.

"Yes."

She looked so full of anticipation, he had to laugh again. "There's nothing like a willing woman."

"More than willing," she said with her usual unabashed honesty that still surprised him.

"One minute." He moved away and opened the bedside drawer. He rolled the condom quickly and returned to Leanne.

She was watching everything he did as if his every action was one of great importance. Something that had been curled tight inside him unfurled like a leaf bud in spring. She made him feel good, and that made him want to deepen the intimacy between them.

How deep? a cautious part of him asked.

He didn't know. It was more than good sex. He knew her dreams. She knew his. He'd helped her when she needed help. She was helping him with the horses and the breeding program for the computer. She was good at both.

When she ran her hands along his sides, then around his hips to caress his buttocks, he stopped wondering about how involved they were becoming. There was only this moment and her.

Her.

He lifted himself over her and nearly came apart at the heat that enclosed him when he entered her. She was hot and wet and open to him.

"Once more, with pleasure," he murmured, and reached a hand between them to stroke the pulsating tip that responded as pleasure filled them both to the brim.

"Look at me," he requested at one point. "I want to see you when I bring you the ultimate gift between a man and a woman. I want to see the passion in your eyes, on your face. I want to see you enjoy this. I want you to see how much I'm getting from you."

"Yes," she crooned. "Yes. Yes. Yes."

They went over the edge together, staring intently into each other's eyes.

"I want to go," Leanne insisted.

Cade shook his head. "You need to rest. You're injured."

"If one of the men was bitten because he stupidly turned his back on a cantankerous horse, would you insist he take the rest of the day off?"

When he frowned at her, she knew she'd won. She pulled on her clothes and sneakers as fast as she could and clamped her hat on her head. Cade was ready before she was and waited for her. Crossing to the arena, she was careful not to touch him. She'd seen women cling to men as if they owned them after making love. She wouldn't like someone doing that to her. She wouldn't do it, either.

Although she did want to touch him again.

"Stay inside," he ordered. "I'll bring the horses in. We'll finish this bunch and call it a day. The storm is on its way. The animals will get spooky if there's lightning."

She followed him inside the huge building and saluted smartly at his back.

He caught her in the act. He stared at her a minute, then a grin broke over his face, turning him into the handsomest man she'd ever seen. "Don't think you'll be able to get away with being smart just because you're sleeping with the boss," he warned.

"You mean, I don't get special privileges? Well, heck!"

He shook his head, ruffled her hair, then lingered, running his fingertips down her cheek to her mouth. She kissed one finger as it brushed over her lips.

"Put it where it counts," he ordered gruffly, and bent to her mouth before she could speak.

They went from teasing to hot in a flash. He gathered her into his arms, wrapping her in a blanket of warmth and the strangest bliss she'd ever known. The kiss trembled on the brink of control.

He let her go abruptly and stalked out.

She leaned against a post, spent as if she'd run a mile. She knew why he'd left. Their passion for each other bothered him. It was all-consuming and way too involving. He didn't want involvement.

"That was a pretty scene," another voice intruded into her musing.

Whirling, then wincing as she moved her shoulder, she saw Bill at the side door, standing in the shadows. "When did you get here?" she demanded.

"About the time the kiss went from warm to hot." He walked over and studied her moodily. "I don't think you ever kissed me like that."

"I didn't," she admitted.

"Why?"

She understood what he wanted to know. "It's different with Cade. He…from the first moment…there was something about him…"

Words failed her. She didn't want to hurt Bill, but neither could she out-and-out lie. The muscles in his jaw worked. She steeled herself for his anger.

"It's because he's new—a stranger, and therefore more exciting than the man who's been your friend all your life. But strangers can be dangerous, Leanne. You could be hurt."

"Cade would never hurt me."

He made an impatient sound. "You've known the man all of what? Barely over a week. And married him. My God, where was your head?"

"Where it always was according to you and Rand—up in the clouds."

He didn't catch the irony. "Yes." He ran his hands through his hair, then put them on his hips.

The lecture mode, she cynically observed. Maybe Cade's attitude was rubbing off on her. She'd never been cynical of her longtime friend before.

"I guess I can understand," he continued. "You were unsure about the wedding. I admit I was pushing you and using Rand to help out. You ran off and right into someone who was sympathetic and, as you said, different. You were vulnerable. He took advantage—''

''Never,'' she stated, glaring at her ex-fiancé. ''Cade was always a gentleman, even when he had to get me out of my bridal dress—'' She realized she shouldn't have said that at the same time fury blazed in his eyes.

''I can't believe this. No wonder he can't keep his hands off you. Why didn't you call the housekeeper if you needed help?''

''I...she wasn't available.''

The blue eyes narrowed. ''Where the hell were you when you met up with him?''

She considered making up some plausible story and discarded the idea. He wanted to know all the gritty details? She would give them to him. ''At a line shack up in the mountains. It was raining and I missed the ranch road. I took shelter there. He fed me and undressed me and loaned me his clothes to wear.''

''I'll bet he did.'' Bill was the epitome of disgusted male pride.

''And he didn't do a blasted thing that was in the least ungentlemanly. Until I asked him to.''

Fury suffused Bill's face, which she'd once thought handsome, turning it brick red. ''I suppose I'll have to give him credit for marrying you. It's obvious he didn't have to.''

Leanne bowed her head as the extent of her lies hit her. Cade probably wished she'd never shown up at the cabin. Perhaps she should admit there was no marriage, that she just wanted to be left alone to sort out her life and Cade had covered for her so she could. Would anyone believe they had slept in his room without...?

She took a shaky breath as she recalled their time of passion in the big, comfortable bed. Nothing could ever make her sorry for that.

"Look," Bill said. "We're both getting angry and saying things we'll regret. I wanted to tell you I'm leaving in the morning."

Her spirits brightened at this news.

"But I'll stay in touch. This isn't the life for you. You're too smart to stay stuck out in the wilds with nothing to do but tend horses and cows. You'll see that in time. When you tire of the cowboy—"

"I won't."

"When you tire of this life," he went on as if she hadn't spoken, "I'll be around. Just don't make it too long. I'm not a patient person, as you well know."

His last statement, spoken in a lighter, almost teasing, tone, spoke of their long past together. Sadness weighed on her. "I didn't want to hurt you," she murmured. "I'm sorry I couldn't marry you. I..."

She stopped as tears filled her eyes.

"Don't wait for me," she implored. "I won't be coming back to Ox Bow to live. Not ever."

She'd never resume her old life, no matter what happened between her and Cade. Not that she expected anything permanent to come of their passion.

"Find someone else," she told Bill. "Someone who will love you with everything in her. For always."

He was silent for a long thirty seconds. "Is that the way you feel about him?"

Unable to speak, she nodded.

His face darkened in anger once more. "Well, as they say, you've made your bed. If you come to your senses, you know where I'll be."

"I think," Cade said, entering with two horses, "you can safely get lost."

Leanne couldn't hide her relief at seeing him. She crossed the arena and took the reins to one of the geldings. When her eyes met Cade's, something warm exploded inside her and the giddy happiness of their lovemaking returned.

"That was a private conversation," Bill informed Cade with a snarl.

"Leanne is my wife. I told you before we keep no secrets from each other." He turned to her. "Ready?"

When she nodded, he bent and held his hands braced against his knees to help her mount. Seated in the saddle, she watched the two men from the height advantage, suddenly feeling very secure and above it all.

Instead of mounting, Cade strode over to Bill. Although he stood no more than an inch or so taller, he seemed much bigger. And dangerous, as Bill had stated.

"Don't bother my wife again," he said, a low threat that had goose bumps cascading along her spine.

To give Bill credit, he stood his ground. "I care about what happens to her."

"Yeah? In that case, you'll be glad to write a check for the twenty thousand you took from her to buy that fancy house in town. She'll take it now."

Bill blanched. "I don't have that kind of money in my checking account."

Cade was unrelenting. "Where do you have it and when can she expect it?"

Bill stepped back. "I'll forward it to her as soon as I can arrange a loan."

"See that you do. Or else."

Bill glared at Cade, then left the arena.

Leanne felt much better about the situation. With that money, she could start her life over. When she left the ranch. And Cade.

On a quieter note, she finished her work. The storm broke in late afternoon. The rain sounded like a shower of golf balls hitting the metal roof. Lightning streaked across the sky in fiery arcs, while thunder reverberated from mountain peak to mountain peak. The horses became more difficult to work with as the storm raged on. When Cade called it quits, she was ready to go.

"A hot shower," he told her as they dashed across the compound to the main house, sharing a rain poncho, which the wind tried to tear from their grasp.

In his room, as he hung up the dripping poncho, she stood silently by, not sure what to do.

He turned to her and studied her for a minute. "You're sad," he finally said. "Because of your friend?"

She nodded. "It all seems such a mess."

"Life is that way at times." He tugged off his boots and stood them in a corner. His shirt went next, then his jeans. He glanced at her. "You need some help?"

"No." She worried some more. "Cade?"

"Speak your piece."

"I think we'd better not…I mean, we're not married, and we're already living a lie…I don't think we should complicate it with…with sex."

He stripped out of the rest of his clothing. Her heart thudded like a lightning-spooked herd in full stampede. He was the most beautiful man—strong and lithe, graceful in the way of a natural athlete. The hunger awoke.

"Don't look at me that way if you meant what you said about no sex," he told her bluntly. "You get to me fast—faster than any woman ever has. I'm not sure I can share a room and nothing else."

She witnessed what he meant about "fast." His body was fully erect and ready for all that they had shared earlier.

"We have to control our urges."

He moved toward her. "The question is, can we?"

She backed up a step. "We can't give in to passion, Cade. You mustn't seduce me—" She pressed her lips together, stopping the words but not before she'd seen fury flash through his eyes…and something more. Pain? Maybe. Was it possible she had hurt him with her refusal to feed the passion between them?

The impression of hurt fled as he eyed her coolly. "Looks like Bill was your conscience as well as your fiancé."

"This has nothing to do with him. It's just that I don't like deceiving everyone."

"Then tell them the truth," he invited. "And while you're doing that, you might listen to what your body is saying." With that, he went into the bathroom and closed the door after him.

Well, she'd made her usual mess of things. Now Cade, who had been on her side—in his own gruff way—was fed up with her.

She leaned against the bed post and pondered Life, with a capital L. Her brother wanted her to marry and settle down. Bill wanted her to marry and work in the office—free sex and free labor, she wondered with a cynicism she'd never before applied to the relationship. And Cade? Well...she wasn't sure what he wanted. And what of her own wants?

Listen to your body.

That was an easy one. Her physical being wanted Cade. The longing was something she'd never encountered. Her mom, in explaining relationships, had never mentioned the ache to be with someone, to touch him and make love.

She had let Bill think she was madly in love with Cade, that she'd fallen in love with him at first sight.

With a tremor that ran all the way through her, she realized another truth: she *was* madly in love with Cade Redstone.

No, of course she wasn't. Really, she wasn't.

She closed her eyes when she heard the shower come on, envisioning Cade in there, water cascading off his wonderfully masculine body. She fought an urge to go to him, to drink fully of the cup of their mutual passion.

She couldn't. Not now. Not with this new worry, this new possibility, eating her up inside. Pain entered her chest and blocked her throat as the realization pierced the center of her heart. She loved him. She really did.

Now what?

Ten

Leanne hesitated upon entering the dining room that night. Besides Cade, Trent, and their grandfather, there was another man. She blinked, taken aback by the stranger.

Gina laughed. "You're not seeing double. This is Blake, Trent's twin. Blake, Cade's new wife, Leanne, who is also Rand Harding's younger sister."

Leanne murmured a greeting. When Cade stood and held her chair, she took her place.

Blake told her he was glad to meet her. When he smiled, she could see the features of the Kincaid clan. He reminded her of Garrett, who, at seventy-two, was still a handsome man with thick silver hair and deep blue eyes. The twins had dark hair, plus the to-die-for blue eyes the Kincaids were known for.

"Fast work, man," Blake said to Cade with a measured perusal of his new half brother. "Wish I'd been here when the mystery bride arrived."

Leanne felt the heat in her breasts, then her neck, ears and cheeks. She hated it that she blushed so easily. As a kid, her parents had always known when she was spinning a yarn.

Cade put a hand over his heart. "It was fated that she and I meet," he intoned with lavish melodrama.

"You got here just in time," Garrett told Blake

after the laughter faded and thunder boomed and rolled over the valley. "The storm is a bad one. If this rain keeps up, I suspect the road will wash out. Wayne said there was a low point that always gave them trouble in bad weather."

"Are you staying this time?" Cade asked.

"Not for long. I have to be back at the hospital in a few days. I was thinking about checking out the local medical scene. Maybe some overworked pediatrician could use a partner." His devil-may-care grin settled on his twin, then Gina, then Cade and Leanne. "Seems you folks are going to need help pretty soon, what with all the, uh, shall we say, population increases or possibilities thereof."

This time Gina joined Leanne in the blush.

"You're embarrassing the ladies," Garrett chided, but gently. His eyes gleamed as he looked at his grandsons gathered at the table.

Leanne could feel the older man's joy in finding his kin. Gina had filled her in on some of the details of the search. The deceased father, Larry, had certainly gotten around. Looking at the attractive Kincaid men, listening to their teasing, she could see why women had been a pushover for their profligate father.

The conversation turned to the ranch and its work, as usual. "How's that shoulder?" Garrett wanted to know at one point during a pause as the thunder boomed again.

"I explained about the bite," Cade put in, "and that you might not feel up to coming to the table."

She realized he had covered for her again in case she decided not to face them after their quarrel. Feeling the kindness of the older man, she wished she wasn't such a fraud. She should tell them the truth before the lie went any further.

How much further can it go? some part of her asked.

A good question. She'd once read that marriage, in olden times, had consisted of publicly declaring the intent to be husband and wife. Having sexual congress confirmed it and made it a legal commitment.

She and Cade had done both.

"I'm fine," she assured Garrett. "A little bruised, but mostly in the ego. I thought I knew horses."

"A friend of mine told me that the only thing less predictable than a woman is a horse." Garrett smiled in his benign manner.

"Female, of course," Cade said smoothly. "It was a mare that bit Little Orphan Annie."

Blake picked up on the reference. "An interesting nickname. Did Cade give it to you?"

"Yes." Leanne met Blake's smiling eyes and saw nothing but good humor and the same kindness that his grandfather displayed. He wasn't a carbon copy of his twin. He seemed a bit more outgoing.

Trent was a rebel, wearing his hair longer than the current style, dressing more casually. Blake was a healer, concerned about lives and saving them. He had a short, neat haircut and wore a white shirt with dark slacks to dinner.

"She was an orphan of the storm," Cade drawled in his soft Gilas accent that was as romantic to her as moonlight and roses.

She glanced out the window. The storm had darkened the sky to a smoldering charcoal gray. There would be no moon or stars tonight. The rain pelted the roof in slashing forays.

"I'm glad I'm inside. The storm sounds as if it's getting worse," she said, changing the subject.

Garrett beamed at the group. "It's good to be warm and snug with one's family gathered around."

His words caught her off guard. Tears filled her eyes before she could blink them away.

"Did I say something to bring up a bad memory?" Garrett asked, seeing her distress.

She shook her head. "It was just…my parents died in a freak storm. They were caught in a flash flood and…and swept away."

"I'm sorry," he said with simple sincerity.

"It was one of those things we all live through and have to learn to accept." She managed a smile. "A part of living, as my father used to say."

"It causes a person to rethink his or her life, I imagine," Cade said. He stood. "If you'll excuse me, I want to see if Watts moved the rest of the auction horses to the paddocks. We don't need to be rounding them up again in case the storm spooks 'em."

Leanne knew Cade didn't care for Gil Watts and not just because of her run-in with him. The cowboy thought he knew all there was to know about tending horses and didn't always follow orders. She'd also heard Rand complain more than once about how hard it was to get good help at the ranch because of the superstition about the Kincaid curse.

Not that any cowpoke would admit that was the reason he avoided the place.

After Cade left them, the conversation turned to the other grandsons and what they were doing. "I hope all you single men will look to Trent and Gina as an example," Garrett informed Blake. He turned to Leanne with a kind smile. "I'd like more grandkids before I'm too old to enjoy them. Don't put off having them too long."

She didn't know what to say.

"Now who's embarrassing the ladies?" Trent demanded of his grandfather. "Having done *my* part to further the family interests, does this mean I get to bask in the sunshine of your approval from now on?"

"Young scalawag," Garrett chided, "you'll have my blessing when you establish a home and quit running all over the country, wheeling and dealing."

Trent locked his fingers through Gina's. "Those days are over. I don't promise to stay at the ranch all the time, but I'm a family man now. I take care of my own."

Leanne had to look away from the couple. They were so obviously right for each other. Meeting Blake's eyes, she saw speculation before he smiled at her.

She returned it, liking him for the fact that he seemed to think it quite natural to meet and fall in love in a matter of days. Cade would probably laugh if she mentioned the subject with him.

With a sudden cloud over her spirits, she asked them to excuse her. Garrett stood and graciously helped her up as if she were an invalid. He murmured, "May I?" and kissed her cheek in a fond manner.

She fled before emotion overwhelmed her.

In Cade's room, which was vacant, she dressed for bed, then stood beside it for a long time before folding a blanket and laying it down the middle.

There. That would have to do for now. Until this farce played itself out.

Cade paused inside the door. Leaning against the wall, he removed his boots and gazed at the bed. Leanne had left a night-light on for him. She slept on her side, her legs curled up, one hand under her cheek.

"What the hell?" he muttered.

Leaving his boots where they fell, he padded silently to the bed and frowned at the blanket splitting her half from his. For a second he was tempted to do something violent such as throw the damn thing out in the mud. He restrained the impulse.

He thought of sleeping at the bunkhouse or the line shack, then decided he wasn't giving up his bed for some woman who had swooped down on him in her wedding finery and thrown herself on his mercy...so to speak.

Did he ask for any of this?

Furious at fate and its tricks, but mostly at himself for not telling her to get lost, he gave a snort of bitter laughter. She *had* been lost. That's what started this whole disaster. He should have been a hard-hearted bastard and sent her on her way.

He removed his clothing, tossed it at the hamper, washed up and climbed into bed. She sighed and said his name.

Electricity curled deep down into his body. He rolled over and lifted himself up on an elbow. "What is it with you, Annie," he murmured, "that turns me inside out and doesn't let go?"

A tiny frown formed between her eyebrows as if

her dreams were troubling. She sighed again. Her eyes moved in deep sleep. Her lashes, lush and naturally dark, trembled against the curve of her cheekbones.

He'd been involved with one bride who had reneged on her word. Why was he bothering with another?

The answer lay beside him, he realized. His own red-headed orphan blown in by the storm. He reached across the blanket, which was laughable as a barrier, and smoothed an errant curl, then watched it wrap around his finger as if it had a mind of its own.

There was something innocent and idealistic about her, in spite of the circumstances of their meeting. She had a stern sense of fairness and a conscience. She was a good worker, quiet and calm around the animals, sure of herself at those times, but not so sure when it came to dealing with her family and friends.

Whether she or they realized it, she felt a lot of love and loyalty toward them. She didn't want to hurt them. Maybe that's why he'd stepped in and declared them married. Only something final and absolute could have stopped the pressure on her. He'd given her a breathing spell.

He smiled as he gathered her hair into his fist and inhaled its clean fragrance. Some breathing spell. The passion had shocked him as much as it had her. He'd known the attraction was there from the first minute. What he hadn't counted on was the force of it.

He turned out the light and settled on his back, his hands under his head. Marriage to the right woman might not be so bad. If it was the right woman. And if he had it in mind to be a marrying man.

Which he definitely didn't.

* * *

Leanne mucked out stalls the next day. When Gil had given her a sexy smile and remarked on the boss's wife doing a man's job, she'd snarled at him so sharply he'd avoided her the rest of the morning. That suited her just fine.

She liked working, and Cade had indicated he had other business, so they weren't reviewing the horses. She'd looked around and decided the stable needed a good cleaning. She'd ordered Gil to handle the wheelbarrow and take the manure out. He'd grumbled about the mud being up to man's knees but he did the work. At least the rain had stopped.

When Gil went to the bunkhouse for lunch, she put the shovel up and leaned over a stall door. Cade had put the mother and foal in the stable during the storm. Now both lay in the clean straw and snoozed. They looked cozy—

The door opened and Bill came in.

She steeled herself. She had known even before Cade had mentioned it at breakfast that the ranch road was closed due to a washout. Wayne had called and told Garrett he was sending a load of rock out to fill the hole, then they would have to bring in dirt and gravel to remake the road.

The ranch inhabitants were trapped for the next two to three days unless they wanted to spent a day on horseback to get to town. Bill was trapped along with the rest of them.

"Hi," she said, keeping a cheerful face but wary at the same time.

"You don't have to tense up," he said. "I'm not going to fight with you."

"Too bad. I'm in the mood for a good brawl."

He stopped a couple of feet from her and leaned over the stall. The mare lifted her head and stared at him.

"It's okay," Leanne told the new mother. "He won't hurt your baby."

As if understanding, the mare ignored the man and began licking her foal. Leanne sighed as a sweet hunger stole over her. She liked children, had always thought she'd have two, a boy and a girl. The perfect family.

She had a feeling love and marriage weren't going to happen for her the way they did in the storybooks. Cade wasn't interested in those things, at least not with her, and no one else would please her heart.

Her foolish heart. It had been getting her into trouble all her life. She followed where it led. All those dreams it had dangled before her had led to nothing but trouble, for her and everyone she knew.

If she'd used her head, she would be married to Bill right now and settled in a nice house in a nice suburb with nice people for neighbors. Security. Stability. Contentment?

An ache pierced her heart. She didn't want nice, not if it meant not having a dream or a grand passion or a great love. She squeezed her eyes tight. When was she going to grow up and quit wishing for the moon?

"What are you thinking?" Bill asked.

Taking a deep breath, she forced herself to accept life as it was. She had to be practical. "Why do you ask?" she said, trying to be polite.

He shrugged. "It doesn't matter."

"You've never asked me anything like that before. I wondered why you did now."

"Don't be silly—" He stopped abruptly and looked apologetic. "Maybe I didn't. I guess I thought I knew you. I guess I was wrong."

To her amazement, she saw interest in his eyes, that of a male for a woman who was new, maybe a little mysterious. Or that of a male who saw another interested male and wondered what he had missed. She wondered when she had become so cynical. Since being around Cade, the answer came to her.

"It's too late to ask now," she said.

He looped his arms over the stall siding and stared moodily at the horses. "I know. You chose Kincaid."

"Redstone," she corrected. "His legal name is Redstone. He wants it to stay that way."

"But he's going to have all the privileges of the Kincaid name—a big ranch, money, even his own line of horses, according to Rand. Is that what attracted you to him so fast? That he's going to have a big fine ranch and a big fine house to go along with it?"

His accusation hurt. Once she would have tried to explain herself and justify why she'd done what she did. Now she knew it was too late. She no longer cared what he thought. And that hurt.

She realized she was losing a childhood attachment, something that had been deeply rooted in her life. Her childhood friend was now part of her past. No one ever mentioned this painful act of growing up, this letting go.

"Or was it love at first sight?" he continued when she didn't answer right away.

"Who knows what love is?" she asked, forcing a smile. "The heart makes choices."

The mare looked up from administering to her baby. She glanced at Leanne, then Bill, and back to Leanne. Her velvety brown eyes seemed to be telling Leanne she knew exactly what love was and would share the information when the stranger wasn't around.

"If I'd bought the property instead of the house, would you have chosen me?"

Her heart lurched sickeningly. She might never have met Cade, or only as a married woman when she came to visit Rand and Suzanne. She shook her head. "I don't think I could have gone through with the ceremony anyway. I'm sorry. It just wouldn't have worked."

The wind scurried about the eaves of the stable. It drove ragged layers of clouds across the sky. Inside, the silence fell between her and the man she'd once thought of as her friend like an abyss dropping open at her feet.

When she released a heavy sigh, Bill shifted and laid a hand on her shoulder. "I'm sorry, too. I think we could have had a good life. I want you to be happy."

She nodded without looking up. She didn't want him to see the ache of unhappiness in her eyes. Neither did she want his sympathy or wise, understanding ways.

Truthfully, she didn't know what she wanted. She couldn't seem to get her life right no matter how hard she tried. Perhaps she needed to start over someplace where no one knew her at all.

"I'll be around for a couple more days. If you need to talk, I'll listen," Bill told her.

"Thank you."

The stable door opened, bringing a crisp gust of wind still fresh with rain inside along with Cade and Gil Watts.

Cade took in the scene—Leanne, looking quietly unhappy, and her old boyfriend, who still had a hand on her shoulder, looking supportive and understanding. He braced himself for trouble.

"Stalls done?" he asked in a tone much rougher than he'd meant it to be.

Bill gave him a hard, appraising perusal. Cade returned the look. Leanne swung around.

"Yes, I'm done." She didn't smile or act glad to see him in any way.

Cade waited for a clue from her. Had she confessed all to her old friend? Was the truth out and everything forgiven between the couple? And where did that leave him?

He cursed under his breath. "Come on," he told Watts, "we have hay to check." He led the way out the other side of the stable, angry and not sure why.

"Nice to have old friends, huh?" Watts asked nastily.

Cade wanted to sock the man. Instead, he gave him a steady stare until the cowboy looked away. "I want a trench dug to lead this water toward the creek, away from the barn and the paddocks where the auction horses are. Check with Rand about help if you need it."

"You going to work with the horses some more?"

"Yeah."

"You ask me, I'd say you're getting rid of the wrong stock. We've always used Western horses for the remuda."

"The line here has played out. It needs new blood. I'm looking at Quarter horses for the working remuda."

"What about the Appaloosas?" Watts demanded.

"They're a special breeding program apart from the others."

"Speaking of breeding," Watts began, "you'd better keep an eye on your wife. She seems to like the city dude."

"He's a longtime friend of the family." Cade was surprised at how calmly he said this.

"Word at the bunkhouse is he was her fiancé. Funny, huh?"

"He's history." Cade raised one eyebrow in warning. "Let's get to work."

"Sure. You're the boss."

The man's insolence grated, but Cade decided to ignore it. He wasn't an owner here until the sale was final. When that happened, Watts was going to be advised to find new employment. The remuda hand wasn't good enough with the horses to keep around longer than necessary. He used old methods of training that intimidated the animal into obeying instead of teaching it to work willingly with its rider.

Putting his anger at seeing Leanne so cozy with her old friend aside, Cade considered asking his brother Ryder to come up and help with the Quarter horse string he was thinking of buying. They'd be green as grass and would take a month of training to bring them up to Redstone standards. Their dad had been a stickler for training ranch mounts correctly.

Leanne was good with the animals, just as she'd said, but he doubted she would stick around that long. A few weeks of real work and she'd head back to the easy life.

His fury mounted. Women always held out the promise of heaven to a man. Then they backed off. So, okay, he could handle that. If she went home with Bill...

He smacked the fence with the heel of his hand, startling two of the horses who had come over to investigate him. He clucked his tongue and they came back. He caught them by the mane and led them inside the arena. Leanne was waiting for him by the time he got there.

She tossed a blanket over the horse nearest her. "I don't think I can handle the saddle just yet."

Reminded of her injury, he threw the saddle on, then cinched it for her.

The bruises had been deep purple when he'd undressed her. He'd been careful of them when they'd made love. She'd teased him about kissing it and making it all better.

Heat roared through him like a forest fire. Gritting his teeth, he linked his hands for her to step into for a leg up. She paused beside him.

"I think Bill understands why I left," she said. "He said if I wanted to talk, he would listen."

"Bully for him," Cade snarled, wiping the tender expression from her face. "Did you also tell him the marriage is a fake and he can get back in the running?''

She stared at him for a long ten seconds. He was aware of her gaze running down his body, then returning to his face.

"I never meant to drag you into my mess," she murmured. "I don't want to hurt you—"

"You can't," he informed her. "I'd have to care to be hurt, wouldn't I?"

"And you don't," she concluded. She stepped into his cupped palms and straddled the mount.

"That's right."

"I understood that from the first." She clicked to the horse and moved off, looking like Joan of Arc facing the burning stake without a tear or plea for mercy.

Damn, but a woman could make a man feel guilty for breathing. He took care of his own mount, then swung up and started it through its paces. She did the same. When he stopped, satisfied with the way the horse handled, he watched her and her mount work as one, their motions fluid and confident.

Yeah, she was good. He'd miss her when she was gone. Her help. He'd miss her help.

And her mouth…both kissing it and listening to her pithy remarks, the way she could put a man in his place that was both maddening and funny at times.

He heaved a harsh sigh.

Eleven

Leanne worked as hard as she ever had for the next two days. She hardly had time to notice when the road was opened on the third and Bill left. He sought her out to say goodbye and told her she knew where to find him if she ever needed help. She thanked him and let him kiss her, but on the cheek instead of the mouth.

After he drove off, she stood by the arena and watched him leave. She whispered a final goodbye and felt she was saying farewell to her childhood and all that had been young and tender and hopeful about life.

Taking a shaky breath, she rubbed her eyes as emotion welled from that pool of sadness she'd never fully realized existed within her until her parents' deaths.

Turning away, she found Cade watching. When he met her eyes, he gave her a hard, probing stare. There was fury in his eyes. When she managed a trembly smile for him, he pressed his lips into a thin line and walked off.

She sighed. She didn't understand him at all.

After saddling the next mount, she put him through his paces, then put him in the appropriate corral. Working continuously through the morning, she managed not to dwell on her personal problems. Lunch proved to be a different matter.

"I've been thinking about houses," Garrett announced as soon as they were all seated. "You young folks might like your own places, those of you who want to live here. We should be thinking about sites."

Leanne couldn't look him in the face. She wasn't a member of the family. She wouldn't be living here in the future. The lie she and Cade lived daily sat heavy on her conscience and trembled at the tip of her tongue.

"Gina, here, can't ride in her condition," the older man continued. He looked at Cade and Leanne. "But I thought you two might like to go out with me this afternoon and look around. I need to get out of the house. Sitting around makes a man old before his time."

A heartbeat passed before Cade answered. "We still have a lot of work ahead for the auction. Maybe after that."

"I understand." Garrett smiled in spite of his obvious disappointment. He leaned toward Leanne. "Don't let this boy work all the time. Make him take some time for fun and for your family. That's the important thing."

"I will," she promised, refusing to let herself blink when the tears that plagued her nowadays burned behind her eyes. She was aware of Gina's and Blake's interested glances and carefully kept on her poker face.

"Did we get any more responses from the invitations?" Cade asked Trent, changing the subject.

"Yes. As of now, we'll have fifteen buyers, plus

the local ranchers who will stop by, probably another twenty or so. It's a good turnout."

"Will anyone want the horses?" Blake questioned. "The string isn't prime."

"There's some good bloodlines in the mares," Cade told him. "With new studs, someone needing to increase the gene pool in his remuda could use them."

The meal seemed to take forever as the men discussed bloodlines and the auction. Leanne excused herself as soon as possible only to run into Suzanne and Joey on the way to the arena.

"Hi, I wanted to ask you and Cade to come to dinner tonight," she said. "Bill's gone, so it'll be only family. Company's nice, but it's a relief when they leave, isn't it?"

Leanne realized that Suzanne didn't have the ties to Bill that she and Rand had and saw him as an outsider. Because of the supposed marriage, Suzanne considered Cade family now just as *she* was considered family by Cade's grandfather. Thus, the tangled webs of deception.

"Thanks. I'll tell Cade," she said without enthusiasm.

Suzanne gave her a sharp glance. Leanne avoided any questions by playing peek-a-boo with Joey for a minute, then heading back to work.

Cade had a string of horses already chosen for the afternoon. She sighed and swung up into the saddle, taking care not to move her sore shoulder too much.

It wasn't until late afternoon that she realized Cade was avoiding her. He'd stayed a careful distance from her for three days so that there were no accidental touches, but now he seemed to stay out of speaking range, too. It was frustrating. She finally cornered him coming out of the tack room late in the day.

"I saw Suzanne earlier," she said. "We're invited to dinner tonight."

"I don't have time." He headed toward the next horse.

"Are we working late again?"

"I am."

"You don't have to work yourself to death just to avoid me," she informed him crisply.

He stopped. The gaze he leveled on her made her tremble. "That's what you want, isn't it? You've made it clear I'm not to come near you. I'm trying to oblige. If you've changed your mind, say so, honey."

She didn't like the offhand endearment. It was said in the tone of an insult, not as a nickname for his wife.

Not that she was his wife, but she was supposed to be. "This is too complicated," she murmured. "Shall I go alone, then?"

"Suit yourself." He stalked off.

What had she done to make him so angry? Getting back to work, she pondered the question until it was time to shower and go to dinner. Entering the bedroom with a towel wrapped around her, she stopped when Cade entered.

He let the door click behind him, then leaned against it, his eyes dark and moody as his gaze ran over her.

Her blood became hot and carried the heat to all parts of her, making her body soft and fluid, ready for him. She swallowed but didn't speak as they stared at each other across a chasm of distrust and anger.

She didn't know how the abyss happened, but she did know the only way to tackle a tough problem was to face it head-on. "Why are you angry with me?"

He shrugged and bent to strip off his boots and socks. "I'm not."

"Don't lie. Please. Let's have the truth between us if nowhere else in our lives."

He tossed his shirt aside, then unzipped his jeans, revealing the top edge of the white briefs he wore. Hunger ate at her as she remembered peeling them down his muscular legs and tossing them aside.

"Okay, the truth," he drawled in a deceptively soft voice that suddenly hardened on the next statement. "I don't like being played for a fool."

"When did I do that?" She was truly puzzled.

The muscles in his jaw moved before he finally spoke. "When you stood outside and watched your old lover leave this morning, looking as if the world was coming to an end. If you want him, why didn't you take off with him?"

He pushed his jeans down and kicked them out of the way. His briefs soon followed. Her eyes widened at the sight of him, naked, before her.

"He'd probably take you back if you apologized prettily. But you'd better act soon. He didn't strike me as the type to wait long," he continued in the same hard and somewhat insolent manner.

He went into the bathroom, parading past her au natural, and closed the door.

She stood there for another minute, then followed

him. "If you think I'm pining after Bill, you've got another think coming. I'm glad he's gone."

The clear glass door of the shower didn't hide his body from her sight, and the water droplets only added an interesting mistiness to his male outline. The painful longing coursed through her. She couldn't look away.

Before she could recover her poise, a tanned hand reached out, snagged her wrist and pulled her into the enclosure. "Cade!"

"Shut up," he said in a low growl and claimed her lips.

The water soaked her towel. When it dropped to the floor, his arms and body were there to cover her. Wet flesh pressed wet flesh. His hands roamed from one part of her to another.

She wrapped her arms around his neck to keep from sinking to the wet tiles.

The kiss was harsh, as if it released the tensions that had been growing for days between them. Her breathing became ragged. So did his. She felt the wild pounding of his heart against her breast. Hers was as fast.

When he stroked down her hip and between her thighs, she thought she might faint with the hunger his touch aroused.

"Cade, we can't," she protested, trying to gather her wits in the whirlwind of passion that surrounded them.

"Why?" he demanded. "You want me as much as I want you. This part is simple between us. It's the only thing that is."

"Because all the rest of our life is a lie," she reminded him desperately. "This…this only makes it worse. We can't keep up a pretense forever. Someone will find out. People will be hurt, such as your grandfather."

The hard muscles of his back bunched and jerked beneath her hands. Slowly he released her. She could have wept at the loss of his warmth.

"You're right. Now that your friend has left, there's no need to lie. Shall we go down and confess at dinner?"

She wasn't ready for that scene. She shook her head. "I'm going to Rand and Suzanne's."

They stood there with the water pelting down on them, their eyes locked in some silent battle she didn't understand. She wished…she wished life was real…this life, the one she shared with Cade right now. She fought the need to answer the invitation to wildness and delight in his dark, searching gaze.

"Okay," he finally said, turning away from her and grabbing the shampoo bottle. "Give me five minutes and I'll join you."

She fled the bathroom, her heart in a turmoil. It took a while to calm down.

After drying with a fresh towel, she dressed in a clingy summer knit outfit she'd bought on impulse when she'd shopped for her jeans and sneakers. In deep teal, it softened the green and added bluish tints to her eyes.

She braided her hair and left it trailing down her back. She added lipstick but needed no other color. Her cheeks, normally pale pink, were still rosy after the episode in the shower.

Cade came out, gathered some clothing and disappeared again. He returned in a few minutes, dressed in a white shirt, the sleeves rolled up, and dark slacks. He wore black tasseled loafers and looked very uptown. She had an inkling of how sophisticated he could be when he chose.

"Let's go," he said. He held the door for her.

At Rand's house, they found things calmer than the last time they'd been there. The baby was asleep. Mack was watching a movie on TV. Steaks were on the grill. The salad and baked potatoes were ready. The table was set with a lace cloth and nice china.

Cade murmured hello to his hostess and went to join Rand at the grill on the back patio.

"Wine or beer?" Suzanne called after him.

"Beer."

Suzanne poured two glasses of white wine and opened two beers. "Want to take these to our hubbies?" she requested. "Ask Mack if he wants another glass of lemonade."

"Okay." Returning to the kitchen after performing the chores, Leanne asked to help.

"Nope, this is the welcome dinner you should have had the other night," Suzanne said. "I want you to relax and enjoy it. Here's your wine. Drink up. Be merry," she ordered. Laughing, she clinked her glass against Leanne's.

During the evening, Leanne felt the deception more and more as an ache within her. Suzanne clearly liked Cade. Mack was enthusiastic about the Appaloosa line and wanted Cade to teach him how to train horses. Everything would have been perfect—if the marriage was real.

"My brother is one of the best hands with horses

I've ever seen," Cade told the teenager. "I'm thinking of trying to get him to come up. He can teach you all the tricks. I'm going to the res to look at some mares next week. You want to go along?"

"That would be great," Mack said, then looked to his sister and Rand. "If it's okay with you guys."

"Sounds like a good idea," Rand agreed.

Suzanne added her okay, so it was settled.

"What kinds of mares are you looking for?" Rand asked.

"Quarter horse brood mares."

"You might find some good Appaloosa stock there, too."

"Thanks, I'll check it out."

Longing welled in her as she marveled at how great the evening was going. Rand and Cade seemed almost at ease with each other as they discussed the horses.

"Say, Cade, do you think I could do some work and earn enough to buy an Appaloosa colt from you?" Mack wanted to know. "I might start my own line."

Leanne saw herself in Mack's unquestioning belief in the future he thought he would have. She'd been like that—confident that life was going to go exactly as she planned it. She would have her ranch, her husband and children and live happily ever after. She sighed as the ache increased.

Cade settled back and gave it serious thought. "I believe we can strike a deal. You work at regular wages until we get the herd started and, after, say, the second year, if all goes well with the breeding program and you do good work for me, I'll throw in a colt as a Christmas bonus. Fair enough?"

"Yeah!"

Mack's enthusiasm drew a laugh from the adults. Leanne joined in with an effort. Watching Cade interact with Mack, she realized how wonderful he would be as a father. She knew him to be patient, firm, and fair-minded from observing his work with the horses. He would bring the same traits to parenting, plus many more.

Looking around the table, she realized this was how she'd dreamed marriage would be, she and her husband sharing meals and birthdays and the other important occasions that came up in family life with others in the family, both his and hers, plus sharing the raising of children in their own core family. And then there were all the private moments to be cherished with only each other.

Being here with Cade opened up all the possibilities. She wanted this with him. She wanted her children to be his children.

She longed for their marriage to be real. Briefly, she closed her eyes and fought the upheaval that threatened to overcome her control in front of everyone. That wouldn't do at all.

When she glanced around to see if anyone had witnessed her moment of weakness, she found her brother's eyes on her. She smiled cheerfully and picked up the glass of wine. She lifted it in a pretend toast and finished it off.

A knock on the door brought the meal to a close. Gil Watts had come for Cade. "We got a mare down," the remuda hand told them. "Might need to send for the vet."

Cade started for the door. Leanne followed.

"Stay," he told her. "You're not dressed for the stable. There's no need for both of us to get dirty."

She nodded and stepped back. He hesitated, then bent to her. Reluctantly she lifted her face for the brief kiss. Afterward her lips burned with unappeased hunger.

"Okay if I finish the movie?" Mack wanted to know.

"Sure," Suzanne said. "I'm going to bathe the baby, then I'll serve coffee," she told Leanne and Rand.

"I want to talk to you," Rand said when they were alone in the dining room. He took a seat next to her and refilled their wineglasses. "This is hard to say."

She nodded and prepared for a lecture.

"I've been sort of watching you and Cade around the ranch. No doubt about it—you two work as a team with the horses. I've been impressed by that. I had about decided I was wrong, that you two were right for each other."

She clamped down on her lip, not sure where this conversation was going or what to prepare for.

"But the last couple of days, then tonight...hell, even I can tell something is wrong."

"Rand—"

"Let me finish. Please."

She waited, every nerve in her body tightening with unbearable tension.

"I wanted to tell you that if things aren't working out, I'll stand behind you."

Puzzled, she stared at him.

"It's your call, but whatever your decision, I'll back you up. What I'm saying is, if you want to leave

Cade, if you've made a mistake, don't be too proud to come to me, to us. Suzanne and I are family. We'll stand behind you if the decision to marry Cade needs to be…rectified.''

"Divorce," she murmured.

"Yes. Like I said, it's your decision. I know you've felt I pushed things on you in the past. I'm trying not to do that, but I could see the tension between the two of you. And, I think, the unhappiness in your eyes. It tears me up—"

She leaped to her feet, unable to bear another word. The kindness and the insight from her usually full-speed-ahead sibling only added to the pain and confusion that whirled inside her.

"Rand, don't," she pleaded. "Don't worry about me. I'm fine. Really."

This was such a blatant lie even Rand caught it. He shook his head and laid a comforting hand on her shoulder.

"You're my little sis, the baby, the sweetest thing that ever happened in our family. Maybe we all spoiled you, but you were so loving and cheerful, it was hard not to. And maybe I have been overprotective, but I love you."

She laid her cheek against his hand. "I know, big brother," she whispered. "I love you, too."

"I want you to have the kind of marriage Suzanne and I have. I never thought to find anything like this, didn't even know it existed. Now she and Joey are my life. I'd make any sacrifice for them. I want you to have that kind of love from your husband. We all make mistakes. You don't have to stay with him if that's the case. Daisy and Suzanne and I will help you start a new life.''

Nodding, she pressed a hand against her heart as the ache inside grew like a whirlwind. ''Tell Suzanne the dinner was great. I loved being with all of you. I'm going home now. I...need to be alone.''

The worry showing in his eyes, Rand walked her to the door and saw her off. She was thankful when the darkness enclosed her and she didn't have to keep up the pretense anymore. The great irony in the situation wasn't that she wanted to leave Cade or the marriage. She wanted him. She wanted the marriage to be *real*.

In Cade's room, she looked at the big bed, at the evidence of their both living there—clothing and books and personal items mingled in the closet and furniture. She bit her lip and shook her head, but that didn't help. She couldn't stay there, not tonight, not feeling as she did.

If she stayed, she would turn to Cade, needing his warmth, his soothing caresses that made her believe everything might work out. They would make love.

That would only increase the longing...and the pain when she had to leave. She had to think, to sort through the mess and figure out how to make it right, to find the courage to tell the truth and apologize for lying to everyone, especially Rand and Garrett.

Changing her clothes and grabbing a warm jacket, she jammed on her hat and went outside, not sure where to go. The answer came to her. She knew where she had to go to make a decision. Back to the beginning.

* * *

Cade was dead tired when he got in at one in the morning. The mare had died, but they had saved the colt. He'd managed to get the mare with the new filly to accept the baby and feed it. That was one less worry.

Pausing outside the door, he removed his boots and set them next to the entrance. He entered the room as quietly as he could. He'd taken to arriving at very late hours so he didn't have to face the temptation of his wife preparing for bed. Such as earlier that evening when he'd dragged her into the shower with him, unable to resist.

He automatically gazed at the bed as he did every night. It was empty.

"What the hell?" he muttered.

He could see through the partially open door that the bathroom was dark. He strode through to the office. She wasn't there, either.

Seething, he checked the kitchen and den and all the other vacant rooms in the house. She wasn't in any of them.

Heading outside, he tugged on his boots and walked across to the bunkhouse. She wasn't in any of the downstairs rooms. He paused at the steps. She wouldn't have gone up there where the single men were.

Going outside, he ignored the caress of the zephyr wind and the endless twinkling of the stars, the soft shine of the moon on the landscape. The foreman's house was totally dark, except for the outside light that came on at dusk and went off at dawn.

Was she there? Probably.

He gritted his teeth. There was no way he was going to wait until morning to find out. He stalked up the road and knocked on the door.

Rand appeared in a minute, dressed in hastily donned jeans and nothing else. "What is it?" he asked irritably.

"Leanne. Is she here with you?"

Rand stared at him blankly. "Leanne? She's not with you?"

Cade glared at him for asking a stupid question. "She's not at the main house or the bunkhouse. Did you say something to her?"

"Me?"

"She ran away from her wedding because of the pressure you put on her. Did you say something to her tonight?"

The brother grimaced, then nodded. "I thought she looked unhappy. She didn't say much. I told her if she wanted to…well, in so many words, I said if she wanted to divorce you and start over, I'd help in any way I could. But I also said it was her decision," he added defensively.

Cade muttered an expletive. "Where would she have gone?" he asked, speaking more to himself than the nitwit of a brother who didn't get the half of it when it came to his sister and her feelings. "I know." He turned back toward the bunkhouse.

"Where are you going?"

"To see if her car is gone. I should have checked that right off. Then I'm going after her."

"Give me a minute to get dressed—"

"Alone," Cade called over his shoulder.

The compact car wasn't in its space. Cursing, Cade dashed to his truck and took off at a decent clip considering the way he felt. He drove carefully to the mining road and toward the dangerous ridge.

If the recent rains had undercut the road, she could have fallen into the ravine. The road was intact. From the headlights, he could see tire tracks in the soft ground.

Relief spread through him. Yeah, she was here.

He arrived without mishap thirty minutes later, a slow, agonizing, temper-building thirty minutes.

Her car was under the oak at the end of the road. He parked beside it and got out. Stretching his tired shoulder muscles, he crossed the clearing and entered without knocking.

He spotted her form huddled on the lower bunk where she'd slept on the aborted wedding night. He found a match and lit the lantern. Holding it over her, he bent and peered at her face.

She'd been crying. The dark lashes had dried into spiky crescents shadowing her cheeks. He pushed back the tangled curls at her temple and let her warmth seep into him.

He realized how worried he'd been.

Placing the lamp on the table, he sat on the edge of the bunk and removed his boots. He stretched out beside her.

"Move over, Leanne, I need some room."

He wasn't going to give her a chance to wake up and sneak out without his knowing about it. And if he didn't get some sleep soon, he was going to drop in his tracks. He hadn't had a night's rest in two weeks. He sighed, slipped under the blanket with her and wrapped an arm over her waist.

Just before he went to sleep, he felt her nose against

his neck. She snuggled close, sighed and became still.
His body stirred hungrily.

"Later," he promised, determined that it would be
so, and fell over the edge toward sleep.

Twelve

Leanne woke to incredible warmth. She opened her eyes in shock. Cade sat beside her on the bunk. His hands were touching her, rubbing over her.

"Good morning," he said. He leaned over her and kissed along her jaw.

"What are you doing here?"

"Where else would I be? I came to check on you. Since you were sleeping peacefully, I decided to join you."

"You slept here? With me?" She looked at the window. Dawn was breaking.

"Yes. I've made coffee. You want a cup?"

"Please." So last night, when she'd felt his arms around her, hadn't been a dream.

He brought a steaming cup to her, then resumed his place on the bed, his hip against hers as she sat up. He rested a hand on her thigh as he drank from a chipped mug.

Tingles radiated from the point of contact. She moved over, away from that enticing warmth. When she met his eyes, she was consumed by the fire in his. She drank the hot coffee quickly, feeling its heat all the way to her stomach. Every part of her tensed.

She couldn't look away. The need was too strong,

too urgent. Her body made demands good sense couldn't overrule.

"Tell me no," he said in a deep, gravely baritone, "and try to sound as if you mean it, then I'll leave."

The hunger was in her, too, and she couldn't deny it. Like the sweet breath of summer on the morning breeze, it filled her with a yearning to taste life at its fullest, to sample this passionate delight once more, to share all that was her with him the man she loved.

She licked her lips and, reaching down, set the mug on the floor. He placed his there, too.

When he bent to her, she lifted to him, settling her arms around his strong shoulders, absorbing his passion into herself and giving hers to him.

He took it hungrily, moving over her lips in hot need, his hands fierce and tender on her as he glided beneath the sweat suit. His mouth ravaged hers, a honeyed invasion of flesh to flesh.

"Cade," she whispered.

"Yes?" He deposited a string of kisses down her neck.

"Nothing. Just...Cade."

His eyes speared into hers when he lifted his head. His smile was mocking, but it was directed at the two of them, perhaps at the passion neither could deny, or at the tricks of the gods on mortals. It didn't matter. Nothing did, but the moment and this searing magic.

"You make me burn," she told him. "It's so odd."

"You make me ache. And there's nothing odd about it. This is nature, raw, primitive, in the buff. Male and female, drawn to each other, just as we are."

He cupped both her breasts in his hands and fondled them while his eyes ate her up. She reached for his shirt and opened the buttons.

"Did you sleep in your clothes?"

"Yes. In case you decided to throw me out of the cabin in the wee hours of the morning."

"Would you have gone?"

"If you'd told me to, yes."

His eyes held hers steadily, and she knew he was telling the truth. He listened to her. It was that simple and that complicated between them.

She pushed his shirt aside and ran her hands over his torso. "I love touching you. I've never thought much about it before, about touching and all that."

"Another natural thing. The most natural thing in the world." He lifted her shirt. "Take this off. I need to see you."

Her breath caught as he lifted her sweatshirt over her head and tossed it aside, his eyes taking in every inch of her. He stretched out over her and, resting on his elbows, nuzzled her breasts. He leisurely kissed his way from one peak to the other.

"I can't...there's too much feeling. It's painful to want this much, to need like this. I didn't know it was possible to need someone until I ached with it."

"It's new to me, too. And as painful."

"Is it?" She couldn't help the wonder in her voice.

"Yes." He caught a handful of her hair. Sliding forward on his arms, he moved his legs over hers until he nestled between her thighs. "I think of you and need overwhelms my good intentions. And then I'm angry."

"Don't—"

"Not with you. With myself. Because I can't stop

the hunger or control it. Because my body goes hard and stays that way until I want to punch something if I can't have you. Only you."

"I know," she soothed. "I know that ache."

She laid her hands on each side of his perplexed, scowling face. With the greatest tenderness she'd ever felt, she kissed him on the mouth, taking his lips the way he took hers, stroking and coaxing them until he opened to her.

The sweet heat inside his mouth delighted her. It fed her own passion as if it were rose oil, made at great expense for magic Aladdin lanterns and given only to a few.

He shifted, rubbing methodically over and over against her thighs, against that place of aching need. With one hand, he explored down her side and slipped into the waistband of her sweats. He caressed her hip, her thigh, then raked his fingertips through the springy mound at the joining of her legs.

She arched into his touch like a cat. She gave a half sigh, half moan of impatience.

"Just feel," he invited, taking the kiss from her and delving into her mouth, demanding the sensual play of tongue against tongue.

He caressed her more intimately, finding the dewy warmth that told him without her saying a word how ready she was for him. Her heart skipped, then thudded. The tension was unbearable, sweeping over them in waves, sending shivers over her, shudders through him.

"Get them off," he urged raggedly. "Now!"

When he lifted his weight on his hands, she peeled off the sweats. He unfastened the jeans.

"Back pocket," he said, and clenched his jaws like a desperate man.

With shaking hands, she found his wallet while he pushed the pants down his legs.

"Inside."

She found the foil packet and tore it open. Pushing the briefs off his hips, she reached for him. He closed his hand over hers, then swung his legs off the bunk. Kicking his clothing aside, he took care of the protection, then lifted her with hands on her waist.

Seeing his intent, she straddled him, sinking down on the rigid staff with a moan of pleasure. Pressing her back a bit, he dipped his head and took her nipple in his mouth, holding it gently between his lips and flicking the tip with his tongue. His hands roamed her hips and waist.

With hands on his shoulders, she began to move slowly at first, then faster as the heat built inside her. Unable to stand so much sensation, she collapsed against his chest and buried her face in his neck.

"So good," she whispered, placing kisses on his damp skin. "It's so good. With you. Like this."

With his hands and his mouth, with the powerful answering thrusts of his body, he exchanged pleasure with her. Every facet of her mind, body and heart was caught up in the sharing of bliss.

When the release came, it was overwhelming. She tensed, then gave a long, low cry as wave after wave of ecstasy washed over her. She heard his deep, guttural exclamation at the same moment.

Sliding a hand under her and one at her shoulders, he turned them, still joined, and lay her on the bed, then he moved in her until the last drop of hunger was fed. With a low groan of sensual relief, he rested, his head beside hers on the pillow, his body covering hers.

It was several minutes before either of them could move. He finally stretched out beside her, one arm over her waist. She felt his kiss on her temple and his fingers idly smoothing her hair.

The beauty of making love, with all its passionate moans and panting endearments, its hunger and raging need, came over her. The wonder of it, this miraculous joining, this sharing of the most intense pleasure she'd ever known, made her want to weep. That and the fact that it couldn't be shared forever between them when she wanted it to be.

She took a calming breath and sat up. He rubbed her back in small circles. "We'd better get to the ranch," she said. "They'll be wondering about us."

To go back was to face reality. It had to be done. She pulled her clothing on in the random order it had been discarded and set her face so that no emotion marred the surface. She knew what she had to do. Crying wasn't an option, although the pain went all the way to her soul.

"Yeah," he agreed, sounding as weary as she felt. She looked at him but could read nothing in his eyes except the tenderness he'd shown during their love-making.

When they were dressed, she paused at the door. "When we get there, I'm going to tell our families the truth."

He turned a sharp gaze on her. "As in?"

"That we aren't married, that you were protecting

me from...from myself while I made up my mind on what to do."

"And now you have?"

She nodded. "I'm going to leave the ranch and get a job." She smiled slightly. "I think I need to let my life settle somewhat before making any more decisions."

He leaned against the wall and pulled on his boots. "We could make the marriage real."

She stared at him. He met her gaze steadily. Joy, like a single candle, flickered in her heart. "Why?"

He shrugged as he opened the door. "It would solve several problems for you. You could stay at the ranch, doing the work you claim to like while you get your bearings and save up a nest egg again. Just in case your old friend doesn't return your money anytime soon."

"What would you get out of it?"

His sardonic humor was back. "Great sex, for one. A computer whiz for another. A hand with the horses when needed. It would be a good arrangement for each of us."

"Arrangement," she echoed. She shook her head without needing to think further. "No, I couldn't."

"Why not? You'd enjoy it. I'd make certain of that."

Oh, yes, there would be the pleasure of sleeping with him, of waking with him each morning, of working together during the day. But... "What of love?" she asked.

His eyes narrowed as he studied her intently. "That hasn't worked out for either of us. This way we know exactly what to expect from each other."

The candle blinked out. She hadn't really expected a confession of undying love, but she'd hoped for one, for some recognition of feelings between them and not just a sexual attraction. She recalled his description of love—of the initial attraction, then the sharing of hopes and dreams, of disappointments and all the little things that went into living a lifetime together.

If they married, would love follow?

"I won't settle for less than a great love when I marry," she said. "Without that, it wouldn't work. I've learned that lesson if nothing else during the past two weeks."

She smiled at the irony of finding a great love only to discover it wasn't hers, after all. The smile wavered, and she had to look away from his silent perusal.

He caught her chin in his hand, forcing her to look at him. She met his dark gaze steadily. She could see the fires of anger smoldering inside him, but she refused to give in to another male who thought he could provide the answers to her future. Only she knew her heart...at long last. Her foolish, foolish heart.

"Grow up, little girl," he advised.

"I have, Cade." She shook her head. "People say things like that when they think dreams are impossible. I've not given up on my dreams. Not yet."

"What good have your dreams done you in the past, except get you hurt?"

She traced a finger down his lean cheek and across his sensuous mouth that could bring her to ecstasy with his kisses. To marry without love would be to cheat them both. She would wait. "Someday," she whispered, "someday some man will love me as I love him."

"Fantasy," he scoffed, but gently. "We have something good together. I'm willing to work at it."

"I won't live another lie," she said, "pretending to everyone that we're happily married. It's better if I go away and think about my life. And someday find that great love my heart demands."

And maybe she would. But right now, it hurt to think of leaving. Deep inside where love dwells, it hurt.

She knew she would forever compare other men to this one. She would listen to their laughter and hear his. She would watch them with others, with children and animals, and think of him. She would taste their kisses and she would remember his.

"Or else I'll be an old maid," she added with a forced laugh. "A cowhand retired to the kitchen, like Cookie."

He frowned as if he was going to argue, then he nodded, turned and walked out. She went to her car and headed for the ranch, Cade's pickup behind her all the way.

She parked and climbed out of the compact. Reality check, she reminded herself, feeling as if she was marching to the firing line.

Cade fell into step beside her. "Who first?" he asked.

"Your grandfather. Then Rand and Suzanne."

"Okay. Let's go."

"You don't have to go with me. I started this whole farce. I'll finish it."

"I'm in as deep as you. I was the one who declared

we were married. We'll face the music together, Annie."

"Thanks, Daddy Warbucks," she replied, falling in with his sardonic attitude. She quickened her step. "Let's get it over with."

It was worse than she'd thought it would be, Leanne realized upon entering the great room. Garrett was there. Also, Wayne Kincaid, plus the three Remmingtons—Blake, Trent and Gina.

"This makes it simple," Cade murmured to her. "We can get them all with one shot."

She nodded fatalistically and walked into the room. The conversation stopped abruptly. Garrett smiled benignly. "Well, you two are back."

"Yes." She felt Cade's warmth at her back and instinctively leaned toward it. His hand settled at her waist. "We have something to say. A confession."

She felt the force of all those blue Kincaid eyes as if they were the sapphire lasers she'd heard about.

"Cade and I...we're not married. He...it was a cover for me. So that my family wouldn't pressure me into a marriage I wasn't sure of or ready for."

"To give Leanne time to think through her situation and decide her own fate," Cade put in smoothly. "Now that the former fiancé is gone, we can come clean."

"Since my brother has accepted I'm not going to marry his best friend," she added, "there's no need to continue the fake marriage." She met Garrett's eyes. "I'm sorry we lied to you. I felt terrible about it, but there didn't seem any other way at the time."

She fell silent and waited for his outrage and condemnation. She hated losing his good opinion of her.

Another hurtful memory to add to the rest.

She stood still when he rose and came to her. To her shock, he took her hand and kissed it. "Thank you for confiding in us." His shrewd gaze took in the distress she couldn't completely hide. "What are your plans now?"

"I'm leaving the ranch. I need to get a job and to be by myself for a while. To think things through."

"A wise decision. We'll miss you. Perhaps you'll visit later, after you're settled."

He was so kind she could hardly bare it. Raising on tiptoe, she kissed his cheek and murmured, "Thank you. Thank you all," she said to the group, then turned and left.

Outside, Cade caught her hand and gave it a squeeze before dropping it. "You did good," he said quietly.

"It's harder than I thought." She sighed. "One down, one to go."

"Courage," he murmured when she knocked and they entered the foreman's house.

Rand was in the kitchen, talking on the phone to a supplier who hadn't delivered. He finished and hung up.

"Hi," he said on a cautious note, as if unsure how to proceed.

She went to him. "Thank you for being a wonderful brother," she began. "Confession is good for the soul, they say, so Cade and I have come to set the record straight." She told him of the lie and why.

"So, you two aren't married?" He looked from one

to the other, a frown cutting a deep line over the bridge of his nose. "But you stayed together at the main house."

Cade stepped toward Leanne, reminding her of his support. "It would have looked rather odd if we hadn't," he informed Rand coolly.

Her brother looked as if he would say more, but Cade sent him a warning glance. After studying her for a long moment, Rand subsided into a troubled silence.

She explained that she was leaving.

"You can stay here," he told her. "We have room."

"No. This is something I need to do. I'll sink or swim on my own. But it would help if you'd pay me the rest of my wages for this past week. That might keep me afloat awhile longer."

"Honey…" Rand began kindly.

"I'll be okay," she quickly put in. "Really." She stared him in the eye and willed it to be so.

He heaved a deep breath, then nodded. "Okay. It's your life. I'm through telling you what you should do."

"Thanks, big brother." She kissed him goodbye and went to gather her things.

Cade leaned against the door frame, his arms folded, and watched her pack her few belongings. Her other cases, returned by Bill, were at Rand's house. She would pick them up later. Right now she didn't need much.

"You going back to Ox Bow?" Cade asked.

She shook her head. "I thought I'd stay in White-horn. Until I get a nest egg."

His face darkened, but he didn't mention the twenty thousand she had coming to her.

"He'll send it. That much I know," she assured Cade.

In fifteen minutes she was ready. Cade carried her bag and walked her to her car. She wouldn't have been surprised if he'd insisted on following her to town and making sure she was settled okay. But he didn't.

He stood in the middle of the ranch road and waved when she looked back in the rearview mirror. His image misted, and she had to blink several times to see the road clearly.

A new life, she reminded herself. Things would work out. All she needed was time.

Driving through town, Leanne saw a For Rent sign in a yard. She stopped and went up the sidewalk. Another woman, her arms filled with clothing, came up the walkway. The door to the house was propped open with an overnight case.

"Excuse me," Leanne said to her, stepping aside to give her room. "Can you tell me what the rent is here?"

A roll of paper slipped from under the woman's arm and unrolled in the grass. Leanne recognized the drawings as a topography map. Her father had used them to find arroyos where cattle might have hidden. She rolled the map up and helpfully stuck it back in place.

The other woman muttered a thanks and stared at Leanne suspiciously. She was pretty, although too thin. Her platinum hair was dark at the roots and cut rather short. Although her makeup was smudged, bold color highlighted her prominent cheekbones and outlined her eyes, giving the young woman a dramatic appearance.

"I'm Leanne Harding," Leanne said after the silence became too long. "I'm looking for a place to stay."

The woman hesitated, then shrugged. "I'm Audra Westwood. I just broke up with my boyfriend; otherwise, I wouldn't be moving in here. I don't intend to stay long."

"I'm sorry," Leanne murmured sympathetically.

"It doesn't matter," Audra dismissed her problems. "The rent is cheap."

Thoughtfully Leanne studied the place. The house was sort of rundown, but it would be nice to have a friend her own age, Leanne thought. It would ease the loneliness she sensed would haunt her for the next few months.

She was pleased at the rent when it was mentioned. She could afford it until she had a job and knew how much money would be coming in.

"Thanks for the information," she said.

The young woman nodded and hurried inside, obviously not anxious to talk. Leanne climbed back into her car.

She stopped at the Hip Hop Café. There she ordered a cup of coffee and checked the newspaper for ads.

"Cream?" the waitress asked.

Leanne looked up from the paper. She stared at the waitress with a sense of déjà vu. Startled, she blinked and studied the young woman, then realized why she seemed so familiar. It was the eyes. And the shape of her mouth. They were similar to the woman's at the rooming house. The two women could have passed for twins except that the waitress was closer to normal weight. Also, the nose was different. A coincidence, Leanne thought, nothing more.

She went back to the Want Ads and noticed one for the diner. Brightening, she looked around and saw a Help Wanted sign propped up next to the cash register. The diner was quaint and because she'd been there with Cade, that made it special.

Romantic thinking, she chided. Get over it.

She hadn't worked as a waitress, but it couldn't be that different from serving a bunch of hungry ranch hands. She asked the waitress if the manager was in.

An hour later, Leanne left the diner with the job *and* an apartment. Janie, the manager, rented her the rooms over the diner where the owner used to live. Leanne felt much more confident than when she'd left the ranch.

She moved her sparse belongings in, then aired the place while she dusted and vacuumed. When evening came, she had a stocked refrigerator, a shining apartment and a bed to sleep in. What more could a person ask for?

A thousand things came to mind, all of them centered on one cowboy she'd met three weeks ago. She stared at the unfamiliar ceiling and shifted uncomfortably in the strange bed. Life was what it was, she told her grieving heart. She could have dreams, but she had to be practical, too.

There was a line from a song… What was it?

Oh, yes. The heart does go on.

But it hurt.

* * *

Cade joined Serena Dovesong and her son outside the Hip Hop. He'd met her a couple of times through his aunt. Serena was a cousin of a cousin and therefore his cousin, too, per tribal custom.

"Have lunch with me," he invited.

He'd come to town under the excuse of needing worm medicine for the horses. He didn't fool himself. He wanted to see how Leanne was doing. Yesterday she'd called Rand, then Garrett, and told them about her new job and apartment. But she hadn't called him.

It worried him, this need to see for himself that she was okay. Maybe it was a sense of responsibility left over from the fake marriage. He couldn't figure it out, but the need was gut deep. Hence the trip to town that could have waited another week. And the one last night. And the night before. He grimaced. Sir Galahad, that was him.

When they entered the diner, the first thing he saw was Leanne, her lower lip caught in her teeth as she cautiously navigated between tables with a heavily loaded tray. He suppressed the worry. If she could lift a bale of hay and pull a foal, which he knew she could, she could handle a dinner tray.

He and Serena and six-year-old Nate settled at a table next to the front window. "There's someone new in town," Serena pointed out.

He glanced at a young woman coming down the street carrying a shiny, obviously unused shovel. She put it in a car and drove off. "Looks like she'll be planting flowers for next spring."

"I love buttercups and tulips," Serena said.

"I helped Mom plant bulbs," Nate informed him proudly. "Plant bulbs, not light bulbs." He giggled at his joke.

He was a cute kid with straight dark hair like Serena's. Unlike his mom's dark brown eyes, his were as blue as the summer sky in late afternoon. Deep blue. With thick black lashes. The effect was startling against the boy's dusky skin. Where those eyes came from was a mystery his mother hadn't divulged.

Cade glanced back at the diner. Leanne was coming their way. Instantly he felt a tightening inside as if all his nerves went on alert.

"Hello," she said brightly as she set down three glasses of water. "The lunch special is corned beef with cabbage, corn bread and chocolate pudding tart. Shall I get you something to drink while you decide?"

"Iced tea," Serena said. "You're new here, aren't you?"

"As of three days ago," Leanne said with a smile. "I used to work for Simon Legree here, but it was too much."

"His name is Cade," Nate said. "He's my friend."

Cade saw a shadow flick through the green eyes. "He's a true and loyal friend," she told the boy sincerely.

He swallowed hard. He didn't know why the words meant so much to him. He introduced her to his Native American kin.

"We've missed you at the ranch," he continued. "Garrett told me to say hi for him when I saw you. The spreadsheet for the breeding program is great.

I've put in Stepper and Delilah's lines and added the new colt.''

She nodded without comment and hurried away when a bell dinged from the kitchen. He watched as she delivered another tray of food, quickly and competently, smiling and quipping with the customers. The ranch hands at the counter joked with her, interest in their eyes.

He wondered if he was the only one who could see how sad she was. That bothered him. It bothered him a lot.

The rush hour was over and Leanne was on her lunch break. She quickly ate the special, then took her dishes to the kitchen. Coming out of the restroom a bit later, she paused when she heard a sound like a suppressed sob.

Peering around the corner, she saw a young woman on the telephone and recognized her as Christina Montgomery, the mayor's daughter. She was weeping.

Leanne hung back, reluctant to embarrass the woman in her distress. ''I've got to see you,'' Leanne heard Christina say in a desperate and frightened tone. ''I have something to tell you.''

Sympathy stirred in Leanne. She'd heard the other waitresses speculate on Christina and her problems yesterday when she'd also come in to use the phone. They thought she was pregnant. Overhearing one end of the conversation, Leanne thought she was, too.

The collective opinion was that Christina's socially prominent father would be furious when the news could no longer be hidden. For Christina's and the baby's sake, Leanne hoped she was safely married before that time came.

When Christina hung up, she dashed around the corner in tears, her hands covering her face, her haunted eyes peering between her fingers. Leanne pressed against the wall as Christina went into the ladies' room to cry out her grief.

Shaken, Leanne went back to work. She wasn't pregnant, but if she had been, she would have gone directly to Cade. He would never deny his child or fail to take care of the mother. Of that, she was positive.

She pressed a hand to her heart. She missed him. She missed working with him and worried about him getting the horses ready for the sale at the end of the month, which was almost upon them. She missed sharing things with him—laughing at a new foal's attempts to stand, worrying about the weather, having dinner with their families.

Remembering hurt too much.

"That was Christina Montgomery going down the hall, wasn't it?" her customer asked when she returned to duty. Kate Randall, the local judge, sat at the table with Winona Cobbs, the local psychic.

The Hip Hop had a varied clientele, Leanne had learned. Everyone who was of interest or importance in the town and county eventually showed up there.

"Yes," she murmured.

Kate looked worried. "I've tried to talk to her," she said to her companion.

"She needs help," Winona agreed. "I get bad vibes every time I'm near her. I'm sure Ellis doesn't know she's pregnant."

"So, she is pregnant."

Winona nodded solemnly. "I don't know who the father is, but I think he should be told." She closed her eyes. "Sometimes I can almost see him. I know he'll help her."

Chill bumps spread down Leanne's arms and back. She felt very sorry for the mayor's daughter. "Is there anything else?" she asked after putting their food on the table. "I'll bring you more tea."

"You're Rand Harding's sister," the psychic stated.

Leanne nodded warily.

"Give me your hand, child."

Leanne shifted the tray to her left and held out her right hand. Winona took it and opened her palm. She dragged her finger down a line through the center, then closed Leanne's fingers as if she'd pressed some object there.

"Follow your heart," she said.

Startled, Leanne jerked back. The soft blue eyes of the psychic filled with kindness as she observed the reaction.

"You had the answer in your grasp, but you were afraid. Take your happiness, child. You've earned it."

"I don't know what it is, where it is," she confessed.

"Your aura is between the sky and the earth. That's where you should be. It's where your heart is."

Shaken with longing and painful stirrings in her chest, Leanne hurried to answer the call of the bell that told her another order was ready. Winona's message drummed through her head the rest of her shift and far into the night.

The sky and the earth.

She knew where those were. They met on the horizon of the Kincaid ranch. Where Cade was.

Did the psychic mean she should have accepted his offer of marriage?

She shook her head. A one-sided love wasn't enough. She would grow to hate the marriage, herself, him.

No, it was too big a risk.

Besides, he'd already found someone else. He was very interested in the Native American side of his heritage, and there had been tenderness in his eyes when he'd looked at Serena Dovesong. Her little boy admired Cade. The three of them had looked like a family, sitting there and chatting while having lunch. They had looked natural together.

Winona had gotten the vibes wrong where she was concerned.

Leanne climbed into bed and felt its emptiness all the way to her soul. She contemplated the irony of life: she'd run away from a man she didn't love and a real marriage only to become involved with a man she did love in a pretend marriage. It was funny, but she couldn't manage a laugh.

Gazing at the night sky where the mountains met the stars, she felt the yearning rise full and poignant within her. "Cade," she murmured, and desperately missed his quiet presence beside her.

Thirteen

Cade cursed and shifted with Stepper's movement under him. "There he is," he said.

The rogue stallion stood on a rise of land, watching them come toward him and the string of five females he'd stolen from the ranch during the night. Scenting the wind, the intruder trumpeted a challenge to Stepper, warning the Appaloosa he was in the other stallion's territory.

Stepper's ears pricked forward. He arched his neck and pranced excitedly. Cade wished he'd brought a mare to act as a decoy, but he didn't have time to build a temporary corral and wait for the mare to attract the thieving stallion. The auction was set for the coming weekend, only a couple of days away. He had to retrieve the stock and get back.

He worked his way up into the rough country, following the trail laid down by the stallion and mares. He was tempted to let them go, but it wasn't in his nature to give up what was his without a fight.

His thoughts flew to Leanne. She wasn't his, he reminded himself. She had to come to her own decisions about what she wanted. Clearly he wasn't it.

Well, he'd done the honorable thing. He'd offered. She was the one who had refused to make their marriage real.

The challenging trumpet of the wild stallion echoed over his head, startling him out of his musing. Fool, he reprimanded himself. He'd better stay alert.

Stepper screamed an answer and lunged up the narrow ravine. Cade leaned forward in the saddle and readied the lasso. He was going to tie the stallion up until he drove the mares down to the pasture, then he'd come back and set the rogue free.

The sound of hoof beats told him the mares were moving, but he couldn't see them. Following his instincts rather than logic, which told him this was a box canyon, he rode straight toward the end.

The narrow passage rounded a boulder and opened into a small meadow, where he spotted the mares heading down the creek. He realized he and Stepper had come out between them and the rogue. Lady Luck was on his side for once.

He turned his mount to follow the mares and push them on down the mountain to the pasture. "Hi-ya," he yelled like a banshee, stirring the string into a run.

Behind him, he heard the shriek of the stallion as he realized his band was being taken from him. Pulling up, Cade removed the rifle from the scabbard and pointed it toward the rogue. He fired into the dirt well in front of the stallion, but the horse kept coming at them.

Stepper neighed in response to another challenge.

Cade fired a bit closer. The stallion veered to one side, then attacked from that direction. He bore down on them, his ears flat, his neck outstretched.

Cade changed the angle of the rifle but couldn't bring himself to shoot the wild creature who was only defending what he considered his. He fired again into the ground.

The rogue reared up and came at them, hooves flailing, teeth bared. Stepper, raised in captivity, had never fought off another stud. He gamely rose to the challenge.

Cursing, Cade turned him, aiming to back off and gain room for another shot, this one close enough to graze skin.

Stepper answered the pull of the reins. Giving great leaps on his hind legs, the other stallion followed. Cade realized the rogue was going to strike. He saw the flash of hooves, then felt the stunning blow to his leg just above the knee. He brought the rifle up, a thin barrier against thirteen hundred pounds of enraged beast. The impact of a head against his shoulder threw him sideways.

Pain whirled like a red haze through his mind. He felt himself falling and tried to kick free. He landed on the rocky soil with a bone-crunching thump and felt the impact of a rock on the back of his head. He fought off the blackness that threatened to engulf him. His left foot was suspended in the stirrup above him. He had to get it free.

Stepper stopped as he'd been trained to do under the circumstances. He pivoted to face the intruding stallion.

Cade realized the Appaloosa was keeping his body between his fallen rider and the wild stallion. When the rogue came close, Stepper laid his ears back and snapped.

Cade pushed himself up with one hand, grabbed

the stirrup with the other and freed his foot. When he tried to stand, he couldn't.

His right leg was probably broken where he'd been hit. The left ankle was definitely sprained. He leaned against a boulder and picked up the rifle from the dust.

Ignoring the pain, he aimed and fired.

The wild stallion screamed in rage and, whirling, raced off, tail and mane flying like banners, a furrow where the bullet had skimmed along his right flank speeding him along.

Cade laid the gun carefully aside. He felt the darkness rushing over him as the pain ricocheted down his head and shoulder and joined that from his leg and ankle.

"Leanne," he mumbled. "I need you."

He didn't know why he said that.

Leanne sat at the little table in the apartment and read the newspaper. It was her day off, her first. She finished the news, then idly glanced through the Want Ads. There was one for the Kincaid ranch. "Ranch hand needed. Experienced with horses. Top pay. Contact Rand Harding, Kincaid ranch."

She finished the cup of coffee and argued with herself for fifteen minutes before picking up the phone. She rang the ranch office at the bunkhouse. Rand answered.

"Rand? This is Leanne," she said quickly. "I saw the ad in the paper for someone to help with the horses. I want to apply for the job."

There was a second of silence, then, "Look, Leanne, I can't talk right now. I'm expecting a call."

Something in his tone alerted her, "What's wrong?"

He hesitated. "We're getting a search party together. Rafe Rawlings is bringing a team of dogs to track…"

"Who?" she demanded when he paused again.

"It's Cade. He left yesterday morning to round up some mares that got out. He didn't come in last night. His horse was standing at the stable this morning when Gil got there."

"Cade," she said, her breath coming short and fast. "I'll be there in thirty minutes."

"There's no need—"

"There's every need," she corrected fiercely.

The line hummed with tension. "Okay. We'll be heading northwest toward the Crazies. We don't have time to wait for you. You can catch up."

"Right."

She hung up, grabbed her hat, a long-sleeved shirt and sunglasses and took off, panic edging closer as she thought of Cade hurt…dying…dead.

"Hold on," she prayed over and over. "Hold on, my love. Please. Please, let him hold on."

She arrived at the ranch twenty minutes after the search team left. Gina and Suzanne were waiting for her.

"We have your mount ready," Suzanne told her, handing the reins over on a chestnut gelding.

Gina handed her a fanny pack. "Water," she said. "And food, some first-aid stuff."

Leanne strapped it on, checked the cinch and mounted up. "Thanks," she said, and was off.

The trail of the rescuers was easy to follow. She

picked it up in the high grass beyond the meadow and followed them up the increasingly steep slope. The land became rocky and treacherous. Limestone bluffs jutted at rigid angles toward the sky, hidden arroyos suddenly opened at a turn in the trail.

She caught sight of Rand, Garrett, the Remmington twins and another man on a rise far ahead of her. When she yelled a hello, they stopped. Rand and Garrett waved, motioned her onward, then the group resumed their tracking behind a couple of mongrel dogs. She rode on.

Forty minutes later, she wiped the sweat off her face and sat back on her heels. At some point she'd lost the rescue team. Now she'd have to circle back to see if she could pick up their prints again.

The signs were confusing. At a fork in the trail, it appeared horses had gone in both directions and it was impossible for her to tell who or when. She'd taken the right branch into this arroyo rather than the one leading up the ridge. Her father had taught her to do that. When unsure, always go to the right, then you always knew which trail you'd already tried if you got confused. She'd obviously made the wrong choice.

Bending forward, she studied the hoof prints in the dirt. Horses had passed that way recently. Most were shod. One was not.

Odd, that.

She remounted and observed the narrow canyon. It dead-ended about three hundred yards ahead. But there were no signs of the unshod horse having returned down the trail. She didn't think it was hiding. There wasn't that much cover.

Clicking to the chestnut gelding, she rode along the irregular game trail that ran alongside a small wash, empty now that they hadn't had rain since the big storm.

Near the end of the arroyo, she paused, intending to turn back, until she heard a gunshot reverberate between the canyon walls ahead of her. Curious and worried, she urged the gelding on. Rounding a house-high boulder, she found the canyon opened into a tiny valley with a winding line of cottonwoods running its length.

"Hello?" she called.

Her voice echoed eerily back to her again and again. She rode into the valley and called again. When the echo died away, she heard another voice.

"Here," it said. "The creek."

Her heart lurched even before she consciously knew who the person was. She kicked her mount into a canter and headed for the cottonwoods.

"Cade," she called. "Answer me."

"Here."

His voice was so close, she was startled. "Where?" She couldn't see him.

A hand waved above a rock outcropping. She rode toward it, dismounted and dropped the reins to the ground. The gelding immediately started cropping the sparse grass. She rushed around the rocks. "Cade," she said, dropping to the ground beside him.

"What took you so long?" he asked irritably.

She laughed and kissed his dear, precious face. "I thought you were dead," she told him. "I was so afraid."

"Put those lips where they'll do the most good,"

he ordered, then slid a hand into her hair and pulled her face to his.

The kiss was brief. He released her with a groan.

"My head hurts like hell," he complained. "And my leg and shoulder."

"Is anything broken?"

He shrugged. "My pride, for sure. Never expected a wild horse to attack while I was firing shots in front of it."

"It must have been feral. At one time, it must have been trained not to fear gunfire."

"Yeah, that's what I decided about the time it kicked the hell out of me and knocked me off my horse."

"You have a lump on your head, but your pupils look okay. I don't think you have a concussion."

He rubbed his shoulder and leg. "My left ankle is killing me. Got it caught in the stirrup for a minute or two. Stepper was a champ. He stayed still until I was free and kept between me and the rogue stallion."

"I'll see that he gets all the oats he wants every day of his life," she vowed.

While Cade relaxed, she checked him over thoroughly. She couldn't look him in the eye, not after the way she'd acted, throwing herself at him and kissing him as if there was no tomorrow.

"I can't tell if anything's broken," she said. She tugged his boot off as gently as she could. "Your ankle is pretty swollen. I'll wrap it in a cold cloth."

She wet a bandage in the creek and wrapped the injured ankle tightly.

"Help me get the boot back on and we'll be out of here," he ordered.

"Are you sure you can make it?" At his nod, she continued, "Your grandfather and some others are nearby. We'll signal them." She picked up his rifle and fired into a tree a hundred yards away.

Cade chuckled. "For a minute there, I was afraid you were going to fire straight up into the air. I don't think I can crawl fast enough to get to cover."

She looked at him without smiling. "I know how to handle a gun." She handed him the fanny pack. "There's food if you want it."

Walking away from the cottonwood and the shade it provided from the noon heat, she clenched her hands and sought control of the wild emotions that raged through her.

Cade was alive. That was all that counted. Her love for him was trivial compared to that. She waited ten minutes, then fired the rifle again.

An answering shot immediately followed hers. She went back to Cade. "Help is on the way."

"I heard." He watched her relentlessly as he ate a couple of granola bars and drank a container of water.

She sat on a rock near him and laid a hand on his forehead. Thank God, he didn't feel warm. "Were you very cold during the night?"

"No. I thought of making love to you and it warmed me clear through," he murmured in a husky tone. He trailed a finger down her suddenly hot cheek. "I always went for blushing cowgirls."

She managed a smile while she pushed his hand away. "You're incorrigible. Thinking of sex when you could have been dead."

"I figure it showed I was still alive. How about some of those kisses for dessert?"

He gave her a sexy leer that nearly had her toppling into his arms. The sound of horses coming into the valley stopped the images forming in her mind.

"Saved," he murmured with a wicked grin, not referring to the rescue.

It touched her to see the relief on Garrett's face when he saw Cade was alive and mostly well. The men lifted him onto her horse. She started to mount behind Rand for the ride back.

"You'd better ride with me," Cade suggested. "In case I get a dizzy spell and fall off."

Aware of the amused glances of his grandfather, his two half brothers, the ranch foreman and Rafe Rawlings, who was introduced as the sheriff, she remained where she was, not sure whether to follow her common sense or her heart.

Cade reined the gelding close to her and moved his foot aside so she could reach the stirrup. "In front," he said, "so I can lean on you."

He held out his left hand and slid back in the saddle with a slight grimace.

"Hurry up, girl," Garrett said. "Time's a'wasting."

She ignored the helping hand and, standing on the boulder, climbed into the saddle in front of Cade and took the reins. He linked his hands together in front of her, enclosing her in the warmth of his embrace. She set a slow pace on the homeward journey.

Rand told her to follow the creek. It would take them to the ranch headquarters quicker than the other trail. They found the mares halfway back. The band joined the riders and other horses as if happy to see them and went docilely back to the paddock. Gina, Suzanne, carrying Joey, and Cookie hurried over as soon as they arrived.

"We'll take Cade to the hospital in Whitehorn," Garrett decided, giving his grandson a worried perusal.

"I'm fine—"

"Do as your grandfather says," Leanne ordered.

"Yes, ma'am."

That drew a laugh from the other men. Garrett brought a truck around and, thanks to his brothers, Cade got in. Sweat broke out across his forehead, indicating the pain he wouldn't admit to.

"Get in," Garrett urged, looking at Leanne.

She suddenly felt self-conscious. Fate had intervened and let her find her love, but she had no place in his life. "I'll wait here. I want to talk to Rand and…and visit with Suzanne and the baby."

Cade nodded and closed the door to the truck with an effort. Garrett frowned, but took off for town.

"Well, I'd better get these hounds back to their owners," Rafe Rawlings told them. "Here, Freeway. Here, Sonny. Let's go."

The two dogs, panting in the shade, leaped into the back of the sheriff's truck. The brothers shook hands with him and thanked him for his help.

When the small group dispersed, Leanne followed Rand to the ranch office after promising to join Suzanne for lunch.

"What about the job?" she asked.

He took the chair behind the desk and studied her

with a frown. "I'd better discuss it with Wayne. He's the ranch manager."

"You're the foreman. You can hire and fire."

He drummed his fingers on the desk. "We need help now. With the auction in two days and Cade probably laid up, we don't have anyone to show the horses."

"I can do it."

"What about your job at the restaurant?" He was hedging and they both knew it.

"Two women stopped in this week asking for work. I won't be leaving Janie in a lurch."

He sighed, then nodded. "Can you start Saturday?"

"Yes." She started out the door. "This is the life I want. It's as much in my blood as it is yours."

"Yeah. But it can be a hard one."

"I'm not afraid of work." She headed for Rand's house. Playing with Joey and chatting with Suzanne, she passed the rest of the morning with only an occasional glance out the window. It was almost two when Garrett and Cade arrived.

"Go see how he is," Suzanne told her with an encouraging smile. "It's the polite thing to do."

Leanne hurried out. Garrett was handing Cade a set of crutches when she arrived at the truck. She stared at the cast on his left leg. His jeans were cut open to his knee.

"He has a hairline fracture above the ankle," the older man explained when Cade didn't. "The rest— his head, shoulder and right leg—are bruises only."

"There's no 'only' about it," Cade drawled, a grin

easing the frown of pain on his face. "They all hurt."
He looked directly at her. "Thanks for showing up."

She spread her hands helplessly. "I talked to Rand.
When he told me, I had to—" She clamped her teeth
on her lip to stop the confession. "I thought I could
be of help since I'd ridden part of that area recently."

"You were a great help," Garrett said sincerely.
"Here, help the boy to his room while I go call his
mother and let her know he's okay. She called from
Texas this morning and I had to tell her he was missing."

Leanne stood as if frozen when Garrett hurried off.
Her heart was beating so hard she wondered if Cade
could hear it.

"Are you going to help?" he demanded.

"Oh. Yes. What do you want me to do?"

"Carry my boot. I won't be wearing them as a pair
for a while. Get me to my room. Then I'd like food.
The lunch in the hospital cafeteria was already gone."

She saw him into his room and helped him out of
the other boot, then gave him a glass of water so he
could take a pain pill. She hurried to the kitchen to
find food. When she returned, she found him in bed,
his clothing discarded on the floor.

She placed a bed tray across his lap. "Ham and
cheese on rye, potato salad, carrot sticks. Is that
enough?"

"Almost." He patted the side of the bed. "Stay."

She sat on the bed and watched him wolf down the
huge sandwich she'd made. He ate every bite. "Do
you want me to see if there's anything for dessert?"

"No. It's already here." He stared at her mouth

and handed her the tray. "Put this on the floor," he ordered in a husky voice.

She took the tray to the kitchen, needing time to compose herself. She couldn't fall into his arms as if nothing had changed. Slowly she returned.

"About time," he said grumpily when she entered. "Close the door."

She did so. Leaning against it, she faced him. "I didn't come back to take up where we left off."

He studied her for a moment, then smiled. "You weren't so reluctant when you found me this morning."

The heat rose in her face. She wondered what she'd said, what she'd given away during those first frantic moments of relief. She tried to recall her words but could only remember the kisses.

"Please," he said on a quieter note, gesturing toward the place where she'd been sitting.

She sat on the bed again, not close but not out of reach, either. She met his gaze stoically. "Rand has given me a job at the ranch. I want to stay here, but I'm not going to be your lover, Cade. I can't do that to my family. Or myself."

His eyes roamed over her and returned to her face. She saw the hunger he didn't bother to hide. "I've missed you. It's been a miserable week. Lonely."

She looked down at her clasped hands. The tremors grew stronger. She could tell him a thing or two about misery and loneliness.

"When I fell from my horse, I hit my head. I knew I was close to passing out."

The fear returned. She took it out in anger. "You could have been killed. Men always think they're invulnerable, but you're not. You should have taken someone with you."

"She wasn't here," he said softly.

"Don't." The tears that she'd held since she'd known he could be hurt pressed close to the surface.

"Before I passed out," he continued, "one thought came to mind…"

Leanne looked up when the pause grew long. She quickly glanced away at the fire in his eyes. Answering flames ignited in her.

"That thought was you. I had asked you to marry me and make our pretend marriage real, thinking that was the solution to the situation. I realized I hadn't told you something else, something I didn't realize until that wild stallion tried to do me in." He paused. "Leanne."

Taking a trembling breath, she met his eyes. "Yes?"

"Don't you know, girl, that I love you? And probably have since the first moment I laid eyes on you in your bedraggled wedding finery."

She gave him a fierce frown. "Don't lie, Cade. You disliked me on sight." The spurt of anger dissipated and the sadness returned. He wanted her. She could see it in his eyes. If she stayed, how long would it be before they were lovers again?

"That was because of my former fiancée leaving me at the altar," he reminded her. He took her hand and held it between both of his. "I was attracted to you. I wanted to make love to you. Since then, I've watched you. I've seen your concern and consideration for those you love. I've seen you work as hard as any man on the ranch. And I found out something even more important. We share the same dream, you and I.''

His gaze filled with tenderness. For her, she realized. Her heart lurched drunkenly about her chest.

''I think we could have a good life, working together here on the ranch, or another one if this doesn't work out. Marry me, Leanne. My grandfather wouldn't like us to have children out of wedlock. He's old-fashioned that way.''

A smile bloomed on her face. ''We'll raise beautiful horses and babies.''

''Is that a yes?''

She nodded.

With his good arm, he hauled her up beside him. She kicked off her shoes and snuggled close. ''Well,'' she said and could think of nothing else to add.

''Give me your mouth,'' he demanded in a fierce lover's voice.

She lifted her lips to his. The kiss was long, sweet and satisfying.

He raised his head. ''Say the words.''

''I love you. I have for ages. Forever. You were the mate my soul was searching for. You said falling in love was sharing. I want to share everything with you—happiness, the sorrows that will come along, children, a home. I'll even work in an office.''

''Same here. I'd take a town job if it came to that, if that's what we needed to make it.''

They smiled, understanding they would each make any sacrifice for the other. Love was like that. She sighed happily, not quite believing this wasn't a dream.

He yawned. ''I was coming to town to get you as

soon as I could make it," he murmured, nuzzling her temple. "Lying under the stars last night, I knew I wasn't going to spend another one without you if I could help it. I planned how I was going to storm your defenses, seduce you, whatever it took. You made it easy when you came to me. I knew then it was going to be okay."

"Egotistical," she chided gently.

He grinned. "How soon can we get married? I'll hog-tie you to make sure you get to the altar." He yawned again, a sign the pain pill was taking effect.

Laughing, she gave him a love bite on the neck. "I want to make a new dress, one just for us, for the real wedding."

"How long?" he demanded with gratifying impatience.

"Six weeks?"

"Okay. Here at the ranch?"

"Yes. I don't want a big to-do. Your parents, of course. And Rand and Suzanne and Joey and Mack. Garrett and...your brothers?"

"Yeah, we'll have to ask them." He grimaced. "The press will no doubt find it interesting. They'll recount the story of the long-lost Kincaid bastards. It's a story that will probably follow us all our lives."

"That's okay."

They fell silent. When she looked up, she saw his eyes were half closed. "Sleep," she whispered. "We have plenty of time to talk."

"Forever," he murmured drowsily. "Don't tell my grandfather until I wake up. I want to be with you when he gets the news that the marriage is going to be real, after all."

Leanne shifted carefully and laid her head on his chest. She could hear his heart beating steadily and strong under her cheek. She heard a cow low and another answer. She heard the breeze blowing down from the Crazy Mountains.

Hadn't someone once said "It's a mad, mad, mad, mad world?" It was, especially when a person was crazily, blissfully, in love.

She smiled. She'd come to the ranch full of doubt and uncertainty. No more. She now knew what love was.

Yes, she did.

MONTANA MAVERICKS:
WED IN WHITEHORN

continues next month with

YOU BELONG TO ME
by Jennifer Greene

Turn the page for
an exciting preview....

Blake Remmington rapped on Serena's door for a second time, then stepped back and waited. So typical of a Montana summer, the early August night was hot and dry. Unbreathably hot. And parch-your-throat dry. Still, holding the weather responsible for his mood was like blaming a rattlesnake for being temperamental.

Stay calm, he kept telling himself. But he felt hot, edgy, and strung tighter than a rubber band threatening to snap. This whole year had been one nonstop crisis after another. Three months before, he'd come back to Whitehorn because of a letter written to him by Garrett Kincaid—a man who should have been a stranger, but instead had turned out to be his real grandfather. That was the first emotional bomb. Then came the shock of realizing that the man he'd called "dad" his entire life was no kin at all. Worse yet was discovering that his real father, Garrett's son, Larry, had been a philandering womanizer who'd not only cheated repeatedly on his wife, but left bastards in his wake like Hansel and Gretel's trail of bread crumbs. A trail that included Blake and his twin brother, Trent.

Lately Blake felt as if he'd fallen down Alice's rabbit hole—only this wasn't Wonderland. For thirty-two years he'd believed certain things about himself

and his life, and now he'd discovered they were all
lies. He couldn't seem to stop feeling blindsided and
confused. A few weeks back, when Carey Hall Kincaid invited him to join her pediatrics practice, he'd
leaped at the idea. Possibly if he stayed in Whitehorn
for a while, he could glue the pieces of his life back
together, figure out where he belonged, get down to
the truth.

But then he'd met up with Serena Dovesong that
afternoon.

If his life had been blindsided by a few emotional
bombs before, they now seemed like nothing more
than pipsqueak trouble. Seeing Serena Dovesong
again had knocked him off his feet big-time.

He rapped on her front door again, then shifted
impatiently where he stood. She was home. She had
to be. Her aging red pickup was parked in the drive,
her son was sick and it was almost nine o'clock in
the evening. All the evidence added up—she was here
for sure.

He glanced around, thinking that the place reminded him so much of Serena that it hurt. The house
was a far drive from town, chunked down in the middle of nowhere, a private slice of heaven with a rolling, dipping landscape out her back door and a breathtaking view of the Crazy Mountains. When he'd first
stepped out of his black Acura, an Irish setter with
graying whiskers had immediately loped toward him.
A real heroic watchdog, the setter had watched him
walk toward Serena's door and then promptly flopped
onto his back for a tummy rub. Now a cat showed
up. A mangy calico with a crackly purr and a scarred

ear, who refused to quit winding seductively around his legs. He sneezed. Damn cat only rubbed harder.

Stay cool, he told himself. Stay cool, stay calm. Do the right thing.

Blake wanted to handle this coming confrontation the right way, but seeing her place just reminded him of how Serena used to be. A hopeless critter lover. A helpless sunset addict. She was a nature lover from the get-go, the kind of girl who'd run barefoot in dew-drenched grass and lick the rain with her tongue and was just always…happy. Natural. Easy to be with.

Remembering made it hard to hold on to his tight, edgy, angry mood…and then Serena was suddenly there, standing in the doorway. Taking his breath away. Just looking at her made him even more roiled up and unsettled.

The lamplight behind her illuminated that exquisite profile, the proud cheekbones, the tender mouth. She'd undone the tidy braid from this afternoon, and her hair was loose now, a shower of raven-black silk swaying way past her shoulder blades. No man could look at that hair and not want to touch it. She'd never said her exact height, but he'd always figured it around five-seven—tall, yet she was so lithe, so slight, so light on her feet that she could walk up to a deer without the creature knowing. Blake had seen it happen.

And those liquid brown eyes of hers had turned him into butter before. Hot butter. When push came to shove, everything about her turned him on—and had from the instant he'd laid eyes on her.

Still, seven years ago, he'd been twenty-five—a boy, really; a man untried in real life. He should have long gotten over his adolescent hormonal response to her. Obviously he was wrong. But hell, he seemed to be wrong about everything in his life right now, so what else was new?

"Blake?" She pushed open the screen to let him in. "I heard the knock, but I thought I imagined the sound...and then I couldn't believe it was you out there. Whiskey, let him by."

The Irish setter was not only a complete failure as a watchdog but switched loyalties without a qualm. He ignored Serena's command and hurled himself in front of Blake's path, apparently filled with exuberant hope that he'd get his tummy scratched again. Then another cat showed up, a hoity-toity white Persian, prancing around as if waiting for him to acknowledge royalty—or risk getting tripped. Even a saint would be hard-pressed to maintain a serious mood, but damn, there was nothing humorous about this visit— or his situation. "I realize I should have called before stopping by, Serena. But I just wanted to be sure that Nate was okay."

Almost as quickly as she met his eyes, her gaze swiftly shied away. She scooped up the cat, tried to push Whiskey out of his way, and once the whole group had been herded inside, closed the screen door. "Nate's much better. Your stopping by is way beyond the call of duty, but I'm glad you did. It's just good to see you again. I was so worried about Nate this afternoon that there just wasn't a chance to ask how you were, how life's been treating you. Listen, could I get you something to drink?"

"Yeah, if you have something cold and it isn't too much trouble. Is he asleep?"

"Yes. In fact, the medicine really hit him like a sledgehammer."

Again, Blake felt knocked for six. Her easy welcome was just like old times, her natural smiles the last thing he was expecting. There seemed no worry in her expression, no hint of guilt. "Well, some grogginess is a normal, common side effect of the medicine. With any luck, he'll sleep soundly though the night. But as long as I'm here, I'll check in on him—if you don't mind."

"Heavens, of course I don't mind. Come on in."

By the time she'd led him through the house to the boy's bedroom, Blake figured he'd seen the whole house except for her sleeping area. The inside struck him as just as unsettling as the outside—and for the same reason. It stabbed his nerves how much he remembered about Serena, and how much the place had her personality stamp, from the circular hearth in the living room to the heaped projects in the kitchen to the colors, the coral of clay and bark-browns and splashes of natural turquoise. Most people used coffee tables for books. She used hers for a collection of crusty rocks—sapphires, amethysts, geodes, crystals, garnets. All raw stones, nothing made into jewelry, or necessarily of gem quality, but the facets caught the lamplight and made the jewels glow. Plants bloomed in the room wherever there was light, waterfalls of green splashing from every surface. Kids' toys were liberally strewn about.

Damn. The whole place reminded him of how easily they'd been friends back in medical school, the dozens of times he'd stopped by just because being with her was always so...easy. Her place then was cluttered, but always with such strange, interesting stuff, a haven where he could put his feet up and never feel stressed or as if he had to put on the dog.

Tonight, though, he didn't want to see or think anything positive about Serena. Still, for a few seconds, that particular problem completely disappeared from his mind. The instant he walked into Nate's room, he felt an emotional slug direct to his heart.

Even in the shadowed room, he could make out whale wallpaper, the dinosaur sheets, the Lego rockets on the dresser. While the living room had a clay-tile floor, Nate's room had a thick, luxuriously soft rug. And the boy himself.... Blake couldn't see him clearly, but somewhere in all the stuffed animals crowding the bed was hair with a distinctive cowlick, and the specific shape of a nose and chin and forehead. Again, Blake felt his heart clutch. And then slam.

Carefully he tiptoed closer. Nate didn't waken, didn't even stir when he took the boy's pulse and felt that small forehead for a temperature. Once Blake had assured himself the boy was all right, he meant to exit quickly—he really didn't want to wake the tyke—yet somehow he found himself frozen for a moment, then two, unable to tear his eyes from Nate, aware Serena stood behind him in the doorway and had to be curious why he was still standing there in the dark.

Eventually he turned around. He felt Serena staring at his face, studying him, but there was no expression she could have seen with the room so draped in darkness. She led him back down the hall, tracing the long stem of the L-shaped house to the kitchen, where she paused to fill two glasses with sun tea and ice cubes and sprigs of mint.

From nowhere she said, very quietly, "You think it's about time we both tried being honest? You could have called if all you wanted to know was how Nate was responding to the medication. You had another reason for stopping by."

"You've got that dead right." When she handed him the tea glass, he took several long gulps, because he was afraid his throat was so dry—or he was so damn furious—that he wouldn't be able to talk. "Let's go outside."

"I don't want to be out of hearing range of Nate."

"I understand. But I don't want to be where the boy could hear raised voices and be frightened by them, either."

She sucked in a wary breath, but then simply motioned him through the living room and out the front door again. Naturally, the whole blasted menagerie of misfit critters had to follow her. Outside, she sank down onto the porch step, leaving room for him to sit next to her.

He'd noticed her nonstop since he'd arrived, yet sitting next to her was different. Before, he hadn't been conscious of her bare feet, the sarong-style denim skirt that showed off her long brown legs, the scoop-necked white T-shirt that loosely, intimately, cupped her breasts. Her clothes were cool and comfortable, nothing fancy. Only they looked purely feminine on her. Pure woman. Like her. And her voice was softer than a lover's whisper. "You're angry, aren't you, Blake?"

"I'm not sure 'angry' begins to cut it. How about

totally furious?'' He paused to take a calming breath and the dog promptly pushed a wet nose into his palm—as if he were in any mood to pet a critter. Then the prissy Persian appeared and put a paw on his thigh, as if expecting him to create space on his lap for her. He needed to concentrate to keep his cool, and the blasted zoo wasn't helping. ''Serena, I happen to be allergic to bee stings. The same king of allergy that Nate has. The kind that I told you is commonly inherited.''

''I didn't know about your allergy.''

''You had no reason to. The subject never came up in the time we knew each other. But that's not the point,'' he said impatiently. ''Even if the bee sting allergy had never come up, I could see right off that Nate may have inherited his good looks from you, but he never got that square chin or the shape of his head from you.''

''No, he definitely didn't,'' she agreed softly.

''He's my son, isn't he, damn it?''

One word. Again, gently, softly said. ''Yes.''

He surged to his feet as if someone had jabbed him with an electric pole. Somehow the shock was even worse than this afternoon, when, yes, of course he'd figured it out. God knew he hadn't been anticipating trouble when she'd walked in. He'd barely been able to take his eyes off her, so glad to see her, feeling a curl of vital awareness he hadn't felt since...hell, since the last time he'd been with Serena years before.

But the age and look of her son had distracted him. And the boy's facial features had kept on distracting him even more, until even someone trying to deny the truth as exuberantly as he was couldn't bury his head in the sand any longer. Still, sensing the truth and having her openly admit it were two different things. "How could you not tell me? How could you do this to me, to him? Why the hell didn't you talk to me when you first realized you were pregnant?"

Her lips parted as if she wanted to answer him, but her gaze suddenly lit on his face, searching his expression and eyes, as if seeking some way to reply.

He didn't want some tactful, thought-out answer. What he really wanted was to smash his fist into a wall—but there wasn't one handy. "For God's sake, Serena, it's not like we were enemies. I thought we were friends. Good friends. I can't think of any reason why you'd have been afraid to tell me. Did you think I wouldn't come through? Wouldn't marry you? That I'd have deserted you without any help if I'd known you were pregnant?"

"Oh, Blake...you're upset."

"Of course I'm upset! I just found out that I have a six-year-old son!"

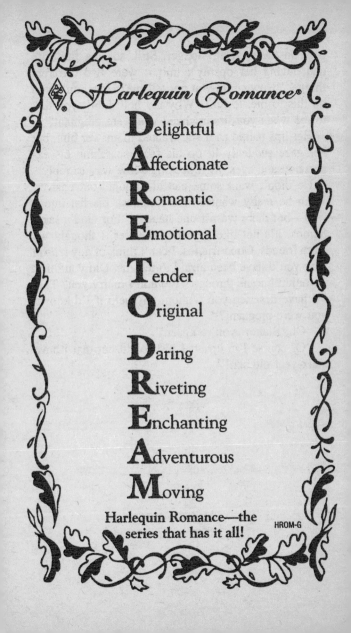

Harlequin Romance®

Delightful
Affectionate
Romantic
Emotional

Tender
Original

Daring
Riveting
Enchanting
Adventurous
Moving

Harlequin Romance—the
series that has it all!

HROM-G

Harlequin® Historical

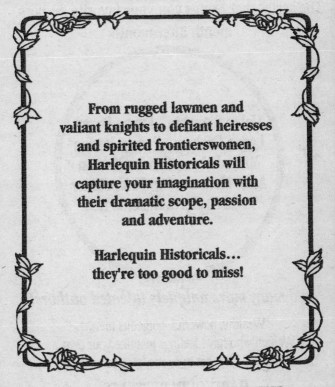

From rugged lawmen and
valiant knights to defiant heiresses
and spirited frontierswomen,
Harlequin Historicals will
capture your imagination with
their dramatic scope, passion
and adventure.

Harlequin Historicals…
they're too good to miss!

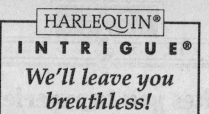

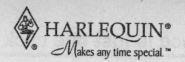
HARLEQUIN®
Makes any time special.™

Upbeat, all-American romances about the pursuit of love, marriage and family.

Two brand-new, full-length romantic comedy novels for one low price.

Rich and vivid historical romances that capture the imagination with their dramatic scope, passion and adventure.

Sexy, sassy and seductive— Temptation is hot sizzling romance.

A bigger romance read with more plot, more story-line variety, more pages and a romance that's evocatively explored.

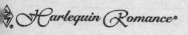
Love stories that capture the essence of traditional romance.

Dynamic mysteries with a thrilling combination of breathtaking romance and heart-stopping suspense.

Meet sophisticated men of the world and captivating women in glamorous, international settings.